MATLOVICH
★ THE GOOD SOLDIER ★

MATLOVICH
★ THE GOOD SOLDIER ★

by Mike Hippler

Boston • Alyson Publications, Inc.

Published as a trade paperback original by
Alyson Publications, 40 Plympton Street
Boston, Massachusetts 02118.

Distributed in the U.K. by GMP Publishers,
PO Box 247, London, N17 9QR, England.

First U.S. edition: June, 1989

LC: 88-083332
ISBN:
paper 1-55583-129-X
cloth: 1-55583-138-9

Matlovich: editor: Sasha Alyson
production and design: Wayne Curtis
proofreading: Tina Portillo
printing: George Banta Company

CONTENTS

The Apartment at the Corner

For hundreds of thousands of gay people in San Francisco and elsewhere, the corner of Eighteenth and Castro is the center of the civilized world. As the most celebrated "gay ghetto" in the country, the Castro is the place where all paths eventually lead — if not for a lifetime, then at least for a visit. Immigrants and visitors alike come for a variety of reasons. Among them is the chance to experience a degree of freedom that has been achieved in very few other places. The Castro is not just a haven; it is an example.

To the casual observer, the Castro is not as active as it once was. AIDS has taken its toll. Still, it remains the spiritual heart of the city's gay community. It is here — or up the street at Harvey Milk Plaza — that gay men and lesbians join hands for the annual marches to City Hall to commemorate Harvey Milk's assassination and to remember those who have died of AIDS. It is here that they relax at the end of the Lesbian and Gay Freedom Day Parade, or party on Halloween. And it is here that they rally to celebrate the latest political victory or to protest the latest defeat.

It was not always this way, of course. Once the corner of Eighteenth and Castro was the hub of sleepy Eureka Valley, a predominantly working-class neighborhood anchored by the Castro Theater, Cliff's Hardware Store, Starr Pharmacy, and several small food markets. But in a few short years during the early and mid-1970s, when thousands of gay men and lesbians flocked to the City by the Bay, the neighborhood was transformed forever.

It was a transformation occurring simultaneously in urban centers all across America, a major social upheaval referred to within gay circles as "The Movement." Like other great upheavals, it seemed to be a spontaneous revolution provoked by a relatively minor incident: a series of riots resulting from police raids on a drag-queen bar in New York called the Stonewall Inn. But the gay movement of the seventies was certainly not without roots, and neither was it without leaders.

Some of these leaders are forgotten today. Many are still active. One in particular, who never intended to become a gay leader in the first place and who didn't even live in San Francisco when these changes were taking place, lived until recently at the very intersection of Eighteenth and Castro. Above the crosswalk, on the third floor of a yellow Victorian apartment building, a gay rainbow flag flying beside the flag of the United States marked the balcony of a man who had a profound influence in bringing about changes which the pedestrians below took for granted. But the man who lived on the third floor did not mind. He may have been less visible than he once was, but it would have been nearly impossible for him to be more visible than when he appeared on the cover of *Time* magazine in 1975, the first openly-gay person ever to do so

The stairs leading to this man's apartment were unremarkable. At first glance, so was the man himself. He resembled somewhat a government bureaucrat with a receding hairline and the beginning of a middle-age paunch. His was not a presence to inspire awe. But he *was* occasionally recognized on the street, and every now and then he would be stopped by someone asking, "Oh, I know you. Aren't you that guy who was kicked out of the Army or the Air Force or something a few years back?"

"No, but thank you very much," he would reply. "My name is Robert Redford."

His name was not Robert Redford, of course. His real name appeared on the scores of documents, certificates, and awards which lined the entrance hall to his apartment. It appeared on an Air Force "Airman of the Month" award, dated 1965, from Clark Air Force Base. It appeared on a Bronze Star, dated 1965, a Purple Heart, dated 1970, an Air Force Commendation Medal, dated 1971, and a Meritorious Service Medal, dated 1974.

His name also appeared on the front page of the *New York Times*, dated May 26, 1975, under the headlines, "Homosexual is Fighting Military Ouster." And it appeared on numerous certificates entitled "Man of the Year," "Honorary Citizen," and "Grand Marshal" issued by gay political and social organizations across the country throughout the seventies and eighties. It even appeared on a Russian River Chamber of Commerce Christmas decoration award, dated 1983, and an S&C Ford Salesman of the Month award, dated 1986.

Finally, it appeared on a certificate from *Nightline* for appearing on "A National Town Meeting on AIDS," a collateral receipt issued by the District of Columbia Police Department, and the front page of the *Washington Post* under a picture of himself getting arrested for protesting the Reagan administration's lack of response to the AIDS crisis. All are dated 1987.

It was on a wall in the living room that the name, if subordinate, was most striking. There, near a set of Confederate battle flags, a poster advertising a gay legal benefit, and a Russian Olympics poster, hung a framed copy of the *Time* cover, dated September 8, 1975. Across a picture of this man, dressed in an Air Force uniform complete with sergeant's stripes and rows of decorations, appeared in bold black letters the words, "'I Am a Homosexual:' The Gay Drive for Acceptance."

The name tag, a small detail, but the heart of the story and the cornerstone of a remarkable and unlikely career, read "Matlovich "

1

A Military Upbringing

That Leonard Matlovich should choose to wear an Air Force uniform when the time came to select a career is not at all surprising. He was the product of a military background. His father, an enlisted man, was in the Army Air Corps and then the Air Force for thirty-two years before retiring as a chief master sergeant in 1971. When Leonard was born on July 6, 1943, the elder Matlovich was stationed in Savannah, Georgia. Leonard was the first boy born in the new military hospital there.

Young Leonard was raised on a series of Air Force bases around the world. In rapid succession, the family moved from Savannah to El Paso, Texas; Guam; Middletown, Pennsylvania; Anchorage, Alaska; Charleston, South Carolina; and England. Some of these places he recalled quite vividly. Others he could barely remember. Because he spent the most time in Charleston, nearly six years, he considered that home, and he identified himself as a Southerner.

Some of Matlovich's earliest memories concerned his experiences as a child on Guam:

"There were still Japanese on the island when we lived there, and they were hiding up in the hills and on the mountains. I remember them raiding the PX where my sister worked, and I remember seeing signs that said, 'Unprotected Area: Stay Out.' The adults warned us to be careful all the time. We kids went out exploring anyway. We went up on Suicide Cliff to see where the Japanese jumped off rather than allowed themselves to be captured. It was exciting. We were very adventurous kids, always getting in trouble for going where we really shouldn't have been."

The war, although over, was still very much a part of Matlovich's youth. On the way to Guam, he passed through Pearl Harbor, where he saw what remained of the destroyed U.S. Fleet there. He also passed a number of small, uninhabited islands littered with rusting Japanese landing craft. Only three or four at the time, he could not help being concerned for the men who fought in the war — and he claimed that some of his earliest gay memories stemmed from this period.

"When we passed those islands, I had fantasies about going in and helping the fighting men who were trying to take them from the Japanese. I also had other military fantasies as well, some dealing with a pre-life existence The first was that I was an officer on a ship that was in battle. I could vividly envision the battle on the ship — the sinking and dying. I also had fantasies of fighting for the Confederate Army at Gettysburg. As I got older, they went away. Maybe I was just visualizing stories that adults told me, but I don't know. They were very real to me."

For Matlovich, the essential element of these fantasies was not death or danger, but the presence of men. He was always attracted to the idea of men in arms, struggling for what they believed against great odds. He had an innate sense of justice — especially when justice was achieved by heroic men in uniforms.

"The first movie I remember was one my father took me to see — a Roy Rogers movie. Some bad guys were beating Roy Rogers up, and I was screaming, yelling, and pleading with my father to go up on stage and help him out. Sitting behind us were four or five young airmen, and one of them was real cute. He was laughing at me, and I couldn't understand why he would do that. It was my first real memory of men — but it wasn't the last."

Like Roy Rogers, Matlovich got into his own share of scrapes during his youth. After leaving Guam, his family moved to

Pennsylvania, where other boys made fun of him for being tall and skinny. Once they chased him, intending to beat him up "for some reason or other," and he defended himself with a car aerial, which he happened to be carrying at the time. Several years later, in South Carolina, his persecutor was the class bully, whom he tried to avoid for a long time. "I finally got to the point where I couldn't avoid him any more. I forget what he called me, but I decided, 'I ain't taking this no more,' and I got off my bike and beat the shit out of him. A couple of weeks later he and his group cornered me and apologized. 'God, you're a better fighter than we thought you were,' they said. 'You can defend yourself.' To this day I am very proud that when I finally decided to fight people like that, I whipped their asses."

Surprisingly, Matlovich's father did not approve of his son's fighting. Despite his thirty-two years in the military, he thought fighting was "a very negative thing," and he forbade his son to do it. He told Leonard to reason his problems out instead.

"But as a kid I found that on some occasions I couldn't do that. Sometimes kids can't walk away from a fight. They have to stand up for themselves, for their own self-respect. When my father found out I was fighting, he always came in and dragged me off, but that was okay, for I got in my lickin's and kept on tickin.'"

Being tall and skinny was one way Leonard differed from the other kids. Most of his fights took place in Charleston, a predominantly Protestant community — and Matlovich was a Catholic. (His mother, who was also raised in the Deep South, told him that when she was a girl Protestants expected horns to pop out whenever she took off her hat.) Not only that, but because he attended parochial schools, which he compared to prison, he was often the only military kid in class. He was bussed across town from the base to school, so extracurricular activities were difficult. He did manage to play basketball for the school team, but living away from the neighborhood made it hard for him to maintain close ties with others.

Despite efforts to fit in, Leonard knew that he was also different in a much more profound way. For that, too, he was harassed.

"It was because of my sexuality. Kids have a sixth sense. When I was in grammar school, they called me a faggot. Then when I was in high school, they did the same. I was always trying to cover for it. But I was also always looking for a special friend, and I guess I paid so much attention to boys rather than to girls that people picked up on it. When I was a sophomore, I had a mad crush on a guy who was a freshman. People called me a queer because of that. I don't remember ever having had a crush on a teacher, though. I was always attracted to people my own age."

From the beginning, Matlovich recognized that he was attracted to other males.

"I've always been in love with men, always. I don't know when I first recognized it as something different, but I've always known that I fit that category. I've always been gay, and for most of my life I prayed not to be that way. I asked God to change me so that I would be like other people. However, the harder I prayed the queerer I got. That must have been God's response."

Leonard could not remember any specific sexual experiences as a child. He may have had them, he acknowledged, but due to guilt feelings which he experienced later, he blocked them out. His "biggest battle" with sex concerned masturbation.

"I've been masturbating ever since I was four. Every time I failed a test in school, I was convinced God was punishing me because I masturbated the night before, and the truth was I just didn't study. I used to have horrible guilt feelings about that, but it felt so good I did it all the time anyway. I never told anybody but the priest. When I went to confession, I used to say, 'Bless me Father, for I have sinned. I have played bad.' I don't know if the priest knew what I meant, but he never asked questions, so I never offered answers. One time, though, when my cousin was standing in line to go in after me, the priest exclaimed, 'You did what?!?' I thought I was going to die."

Leonard did date women in high school, but he never had sex with any of them. He never even petted. Usually, he chose the most religious girls in school so that he wouldn't be pressured to perform. Often before leaving on dates he and his girlfriend would kneel on the floor and say the Rosary to protect themselves from sin. At other times, he quickly assumed the role of big brother so that he wouldn't have to play a romantic role. Other guys bragged about what they did with their girlfriends, but not Matlovich. To avoid lying about what he did, he joined the Catholic youth group, where such talk was discouraged. Finally, if all else failed, he counted on his family's frequent moves. Moving was in some ways a relief, for it allowed him to escape his girlfriends' romantic infatuations.

Although Leonard was aware that he was not the only gay person in the world, the knowledge was not a source of comfort to him. In grammar school, he was convinced that a friend of his was in love with him. "I'm glad you're you," the friend used to say, "but I wish you were someone else" — code for "I wish you were a girl," according to Matlovich. Then in high school, there was a kid in the neighborhood named Scrawny Buck "who was supposed to suck people's penises." Leonard kept his distance. "I was so terrified about my own sexuality that if someone else was identified as being gay, I would stay away from him. I'll never forget this one time, I was sitting with a guy in the cab of his truck when he pulled his cock out and tried to get me to play with it. I was determined not to do it, even though I wanted to so badly. I said to myself, 'I'll show them. They can't prove that I'm queer.'"

Even if he had wanted to come to terms with his sexuality rather than avoid it, Charleston in the 1950s was no place for gay people, and Matlovich had nowhere to turn for guidance. He was warned about a Catholic priest who was connected with the basketball team. Friends cautioned Leonard never to sleep with the man on road trips, because he had a reputation for making sexual advances. Friends also gossiped about a gay man who was beaten to death with a candlestick after propositioning a young airman from the Charleston Air Force Base. Although the airman threw the would-be "cocksucker" out of a fourteen-story building, when he was tried, he was soon acquitted, and he became something of a hero for killing a queer. When everyone said, "Oh, that poor airman, being molested by a terrible creature," Leonard only thought, "My God, am I one of those terrible creatures?" He was fourteen years old at the time.

In other ways, Matlovich's youth was not so different from that of other adolescents. Moving frequently from base to base was not particularly difficult for him. In time, he grew used to it and looked foward to new and exciting adventures. He even began to count on moving as a way of escaping the problems associated with his sexuality — not only his entanglements with girls but also his frequent crushes on other boys.

Of greater concern to him than the periodic moves were his problems as a student. He hated school and did poorly, primarily because reading was so difficult for him. His parents spent a fortune on tutors until someone finally discovered that he had a learning disability. He was not "stupid," as he thought — merely dyslexic.

Despite his distaste for school, Leonard did enjoy a few subjects — especially anything to do with history or the South. His mother's ancestors were some of the original settlers of South Carolina, so he just "ate that stuff up alive." He was particularly interested in military history, and he was involved in the one-hundredth anniversary of the firing on Fort Sumter.

Unfortunately, Matlovich's interest in South Carolina history led him to no real understanding of the causes of the Civil War or its bitter legacy. Because he grew up in a segregated society, he had no sympathy for the civil rights struggle that was sweeping the South. He could not extend his sense of fair play and his love of justice to include blacks — and he didn't even try.

"I remember that when blacks came to the housing area where we lived, we grabbed Confederate flags and rocks and chased them out. I also remember going through the black parts of town on the bus shouting, 'Nigger!' and yelling, 'Two, four, six, eight, we don't want to integrate. Yea, Little Rock!' When Eisenhower came to South Carolina to speak at the Citadel, we hung him in effigy because we thought he was pro-black. And we held meetings to decide what to do if blacks tried to join the all-white Teen Club on the military base.

"I assume my attitude had more to do with my low self-image than with anything else. By picking on blacks, I thought I was making myself better than them. It meant that I wasn't the lowest person on the totem pole any more. It certainly wasn't the result of my upbringing. My mother used to punish me if I ever used a word like 'nigger' around her. She found it offensive and said, 'There but for the love of God go you.' Her attitude did have some effect on me, however. A person I really cared for deeply was my grandmother's maid. Once, when we had just come back from somewhere, the maid was sitting on the couch, and my mother said, 'Give her a hug.' So I gave this black woman a hug and thought, 'Oh, how liberal of me.' "

After his junior year of high school, the Air Force sent Matlovich's family to Ipswich in England, where his father worked as a jet mechanic. At last, Leonard was enrolled not in a Catholic school but in a military boarding school, which made him very happy. His family treated him more like an adult than as a child, and he made more of his own decisions. His schoolwork improved as a result, and best of all, he began to explore places like Westminster Abbey and Stratford-on-Avon.

After graduation in 1962, Matlovich decided to skip college and to join the Armed Forces, against his father's wishes. His father wanted Leonard to enter the service as an officer, but Leonard felt that if being an enlisted man was good enough for his father, it was good enough for him. Consequently, he went to France to join the Army. He stayed only one night. Conditions were so terrible compared to what he was used to as the son of an Air Force sergeant that he packed his bags before signing up and returned to England.

There he got a job bagging groceries at the Air Force commissary. When he earned his first hundred dollars, he was so proud of himself that he ironed each one. Then he got a job working for the highest-ranking civilian employee at the base, a man with no legs, who taught him that disabled people were far from helpless. Finally, in May 1963, he enlisted in the United States Air Force. He spent a day in Germany and then flew to Lackland Air Force Base in Texas to begin basic training. His reasons were simple:

"I've always been very conservative. And I've always had a military mind. When I graduated from high school, I was reading about the U.S. involvement in Vietnam, and I was so afraid that if I didn't hurry up and get over there, it would be over before I had an opportunity to prove my manhood. You see, I had to prove that even though I had strong attractions to other men, I could go to war just like anyone else. And I proved it all right. I ended up spending three years in Vietnam."

2

The Vietnam Era

In 1963, the year that Leonard Matlovich joined the Air Force,
American military forces in Vietnam rose from 11,000 to more
than 17,000 troops; 489 of these were killed or wounded. It was
the year that an elderly Buddhist monk named Quang Duc
burned himself to death in Saigon in protest against the policies
of the South Vietnamese government. It was the same year that
the Kennedy administration backed the overthrow of President
Diem and his brother Nhu. If an idealistic and rather naive
nineteen-year-old was anxious to embroil himself in this quag-
mire, he had far more time than he realized to do so. The last
American soldier would not evacuate the remote Southeast
Asian country for another ten years.

In the meantime, before Matlovich could "prove himself" in
Vietnam, he had to survive basic training at Lackland Air Force
Base near San Antonio, Texas. For a young man used to military
discipline, this was a simple matter. Being selected squad leader
made things easier. And being part of an all-male environment
was even better — although it did occasion "a lot of cold show-
ers." Consequently, his eight weeks at Lackland were "fun, but
basically uneventful."

After completing basic training, Matlovich was sent to technical school at Shepard Air Force Base in Wichita Falls, Texas for six months. Unlike basic training, however, this was not a pleasant experience. From the beginning, things didn't go as he would have liked.

"I really wanted to be a medic most of all, for I wanted to be able to help other men. That way, I could show love and compassion for men within 'acceptable' norms. I used to have fantasies about the men in Vietnam. I dreamed about holding and caressing them when they were wounded.

"Unfortunately, in the Air Force at that time, you couldn't choose the exact field you wanted to study. Medicine was only one branch of the general field, which also included security and food service. Well, I sure didn't want to wind up being a policeman or a cook for four years, so rather than throw my name in the hat and take my chances in the general field, I chose the electronic field instead.

"How I made it through tech school I'll never know, because one of the requirements to graduate was to climb ninety-foot telephone poles, and I was terrified of heights. Once, I fell from a thirty-foot pole and knew that if I didn't go right back up, I'd never climb another pole again. I did it, but I didn't enjoy it."

Climbing telephone poles wasn't the only difficult thing about tech school. Far worse was the hard-line attitude Leonard encountered there. "The outfit I was with was the closest thing the Air Force had to the Marine Corps version of basic training — you know, very rigid, controlled, spit and polish, that sort of thing. It was all bullshit. I was surrounded by a bunch of little demi-gods running around. I just gritted my teeth and bore it. It lasted six months, and I was never so happy in my life than I was when I got out of there."

Immediately following graduation from technical school, Matlovich volunteered for duty in Vietnam. He was sent to Travis Air Force Base in Fairfield, California instead. There he spent over a year rewinding electric motors, which he found satisfying work, even though it wasn't what he had hoped to be doing. He also enjoyed the many friends he made. When not rewinding motors, he was often wrestling in the barracks, something "all the guys did" but which, for Leonard, meant far more.

At Travis, Leonard continued to try to repress his homosexual feelings, but occasionally his emotions gained the upper hand. When he fell in love with one of his friends on base, his attentions were so obvious that, for the first time since high school, others noticed. He was accused by an enlisted man of being queer. Matlovich's response was to get drunk — which he very rarely did — and to make up a fictitious story back at the barracks about a fiancée who died in a car wreck. That's why he didn't get married, he explained, and that's why he was no longer interested in other women. His accuser bought the story hook, line, and sinker and went out of his way to apologize. To prevent any such future rumors, however, Leonard ended the relationship with his friend. Eventually, he became something of a loner, because he got tired of getting hurt all the time.

While at Travis, Matlovich became active in the Solano County Republican Party. It was traumatic for him, as a Southerner, to register Republican. But he was a conservative, and he felt more at home with the Republicans than with the Democrats. He was so conservative, in fact, that he almost joined the John Birch Society but decided against it when a friend told him that it would come back to haunt him some day.

Matlovich's first opportunity to exercise his political beliefs arrived with the 1964 presidential campaign, when he supported Barry Goldwater over Lyndon Johnson. Volunteering to do precinct work for Goldwater by distributing literature door-to-door, he quickly ran into trouble with his supervisors, who accused him of violating the Hatch Act. According to his sergeant, he was breaking the law by becoming involved in politics on a military installation. He was then given a direct order "to cease and desist" from further political activity on the base. "At that point I had a real decision to make in my life. I was so opposed to the idea that anyone in this country has a right to deny anyone else freedom of speech, of political speech especially, that I was tempted to go to jail rather than to obey the order. I decided not to go to jail — but I voted for Barry Goldwater anyway.

"Most everybody else on the base was a Johnson supporter,

but I was a real rebel, a die-hard Goldwater fan. I fought everyone on the Vietnam issue. In fact, I'm totally responsible for the Vietnam War, even to this day. I have to take full blame for it, because in 1964 I was told that if I voted for Goldwater, the war in Vietnam would escalate. Sure enough, that's exactly what happened. I voted for Goldwater and the war escalated. So I guess that makes me responsible.

"I'll never forget the morning after the election. I saw my first sergeant, and he said, 'Ha, ha, you really got it.' I said to him, 'That's okay. Ten years from now the Vietnam War will still be going on. American boys will be dying there, and you'll be sorry, not me.' I proved to be right on that."

Throughout the election, Matlovich never lost sight of his original goal — to get to Vietnam himself. Every month or so he stopped by the personnel office at Travis to put in another request for a tour of duty there. Finally, in July 1965 his orders came through. He was assigned to a Mobile Radar Unit, whose job it was to build radar systems in neutral territory and then assemble them at the front lines. Before actually beginning work, however, he had to be trained once again, this time in the Philippines. That completed, he was sent to Vietnam.

"I arrived in Vietnam on Thanksgiving Day, 1965. I'll never forget it. The plane landed on a dirt runway outside a village called Dong Ha, right up on the DMZ. There were only 150 Americans on the site, as well as a French Catholic priest named Father Veller, who had been in Vietnam for thirty-seven years. I was in ecstasy when that plane landed, for I had made my goal at last. I could show that although I happened to be in love with men, I could be just as brave and courageous as anyone."

At Dong Ha, Leonard installed himself in the barracks and helped to assemble radar sites on the front lines. At night he operated a 50-caliber machine gun — which he seldom got the chance to use. Occasionally, a plane was shot down nearby, and Air Force personnel were sent to rescue the crewmen. Most of the time, however, his duties amounted to "sitting there and waiting to be fired on."

For about two months, nothing ever happened. Finally one night mortars exploded in the compound. It was Matlovich's first experience under fire. "You can plan your entire life how brave you'll be when someone shoots at you, but until it actually happens, you'll never know. You never react the way you think you will. You just act. It's mechanical. You don't have any idea what you're doing. In fact, I don't even remember how I reacted, it was such a traumatic experience. For twenty or thirty minutes, while it lasted, my mind was a blank. I know I was scared afterward. I remember shaking and trying to regain my composure as I analyzed what had happened. Most of us were novices then. We must have been crazy to have volunteered to be there.

"The first person I saw dead was a Vietnamese civilian. He was lying on the ground, and the skin of his hand was peeled back and wrapped around his arm. There were holes in his face where the shrapnel hit. I had never seen a dead person before, other than the victim of a car accident. It made me feel queasy, empty, and shocked. I wasn't prepared for it at all. I don't think you could ever be prepared for something like that.

"I rarely saw friends die, for in the Air Force, we didn't see things like that often. We were attacked about three or four times a month by rockets or mortars. But we hardly ever went out on seek-and-destroy missions. That wasn't our job. Occasionally, someone wouldn't show up at work the next day, and we'd find out later that he was murdered by the North Vietnamese. But that didn't happen often." One of Matlovich's friends who was killed was Father Veller, the Catholic priest. Matlovich had drawn close to him during those first few months, serving as Veller's altar boy at the church in Dong Ha and trying to learn French and Vietnamese from him. Through Father Veller, he met a good many Vietnamese civilians, whom he counted as his friends. But one day the jeep Father Veller was driving hit a mine, and he and two altar boys were killed. It was one of Leonard's earliest and hardest losses.

If the Catholic priest's death made little sense to Leonard, American policy made even less. When he and the other airmen were on the base, for instance, they carried guns over their shoulders, but when they went to town, they weren't allowed to carry any kind of weapon, not even a knife. Furthermore, when they were under attack, they could not respond until they got permission over the phone. The reason, according to Matlovich, was that "officially there weren't any Americans there."

This was also the reason the airmen were not allowed to fly American flags on the base. They responded by flying their state flags instead. Once, Matlovich flew the Confederate flag; a black airman approached him and said, "Here we are in Vietnam fighting for democracy. How can you fly that flag?" It was one of the first times Leonard had looked at his heritage from a black point of view, and he responded by putting the flag away. He continued to display the American flag in the privacy of his tent, however — until he was ordered to take it down and hide it.

After four months at Dong Ha, Matlovich's unit was sent back to the Philippines to assemble another radar site. This time, however, instead of transporting it to Vietnam and reassembling it near the front lines, they took the site to a small town called Phitsanulok in Thailand and stayed there until replacements from the States arrived.

Because he was no longer stationed in a combat zone, Matlovich was able, for the first time, to focus on other things besides survival. He was particularly interested in the local culture. Among other things, he learned that Thai barbers never touched the heads of their customers, for in Thai culture the head is the most sacred part of the body. He also learned that women always kept their heads lower than the men's, even if the men were sitting, and that to sit with the legs crossed and the bottom of the foot showing was a terrible disgrace. Discovering these things led to increased understanding, and understanding led to increased respect. Above all, Leonard's attempts to learn led to several significant friendships with individual Thais.

Unfortunately, not all of his fellow Americans made the same effort. Some were deliberately insensitive, as when they nicknamed Phitsanulok "Piss-in-a-Lake." Others simply didn't know any better. When American G.I.'s rubbed the heads of small boys who ran up to greet them, for instance, they didn't know it was a sign of disgrace. Leonard saw many such examples of unintentional Ugly Americanism; they reminded him of the time he was in England on the Fourth of July and belittled the English for their failure to celebrate the holiday.

Although Matlovich was one of the few who did not treat Thais as second-class citizens in their own country, he did not give himself a great deal of credit for this. Because he was gay (although he was not willing to accept it at the time), he felt a kinship with other people who were victims of discrimination. Unfortunately, he was still unable to extend this feeling to black Americans. Through the military, however, he was coming into contact with blacks on a day-to-day basis for the first time in his life, and he was at last beginning to try.

"Even though I grew up in the military, I grew up in a very segregated society. As a young airman at Travis, I saw that white airmen coming into the squadron were assigned to one place and black airmen were assigned to another. This was not policy, but it was the custom all the same. In Asia, though, all this changed. The more and more blacks I met as individuals who didn't fit the stereotypes I had of them, the harder it was to be biased. I realized that they put their pants on the same way I did and that they loved their families just as much.

"In the Philippines, one of the first supervisors I had, Sergeant Reed, was a black man with a business law degree. He used fifty-cent words regularly, and I used to think he looked them up in the dictionary just so he could impress us white folks. But he really was that smart, and by his example, he helped to destroy those stereotypes."

While stationed in Phitsanulok, Matlovich received his first medal, a Bronze Star, for meritorious service performed in Dong Ha. Because nighttime sniper attacks on the base were a problem at Dong Ha, Leonard had erected spotlights around the perimeter so that guards at individual bunkers could throw a switch illuminating the entire area. On a number of occasions, while the base was under attack, the spotlights failed to work properly, and Matlovich had crawled outside the perimeter to fix them. In spite of the extraordinary nature of this service, the medal, when it was awarded, was for Leonard a complete and unexpected surprise.

After four months in Thailand, Matlovich returned to the Philippines. Then his year-long tour of duty ended, and he was sent back to Travis Air Force Base in California. At that point, he did an unexpected thing. He left the service. He did it because everyone told him he wouldn't; his friends and family said he had a lifer mentality, and he was determined to prove them wrong. Stubbornness thus triumphed over rationality, but Matlovich was soon to regret his perverse behavior. Temporarily, he moved in with his parents, who were then living in Illinois, and every time he listened to the news at night, he knew he had made a mistake. He loved the service, he did have a lifer mentality, and he wanted to get back to Vietnam. After only ninety days as a civilian, therefore, he re-enlisted and returned to Travis.

This time Leonard did not have to wait so long for his request for another tour of duty in Vietnam to be fulfilled, and in July 1968 he was sent to Tuy Hoa, a small town north of Cam Ranh Bay in central southwest Vietnam. He was glad to be back in the combat zone — but he was still plagued by self-doubt.

"Most of my life I wanted to be someone else. I wanted to be born a hundred years earlier or later. I was not happy with myself. And I still felt I had something to prove. I was so dissatisfied with being gay that in some ways, volunteering for duty in Vietnam was like a death wish or a suicide pact. I thought, 'Well, if I could just die, that would be one way of dealing with it.' But also, the male companionship of Vietnam had a lot to do with my going over there. I kept hoping that I would find someone who could return the feeling I had for him. Then maybe I wouldn't have to die."

While helping to build new bases as a member of the Red Horse Squadron, a combat construction unit, Matlovich did meet someone in Tuy Hoa, a man named Chuck. They spent a great deal of time together, and Matlovich continually hoped that the relationship would progress beyond the "buddy" stage — but it didn't.

"I'll never forget, one time Chuck said how much he hated queers and faggots. I don't know if he was trying to deny his emotions or what, because we were almost like lovers, except that we didn't hug or touch or anything. I was so hurt by his inability or his unwillingness to return my affection that I volunteered to go to Da Nang for the last six months of that tour of duty.

"That happened a lot. I developed crushes on friends, and I

hoped and prayed for some sign of love in return. I gave and gave, but no one ever gave anything back, at least not the way I wanted. So then I reasoned that if I separated myself from that person, as I had so often been forced to do in my childhood, the pain wouldn't be as bad. That's why, after falling madly in love with a man, I usually volunteered to be transferred afterward. I saw that the relationship wasn't going anywhere, that I had picked another dead end, another straight man. Now I realize, of course, that many of the men I loved may have been just as gay as I was, but they also had just as many problems accepting it."

In Da Nang, Matlovich resolved to transfer his emotional energies elsewhere for a change and chose an unlikely object — the Mormon Church. Although he was raised a very conservative Catholic, his feelings for the church changed as a result of Vatican II. He resented hearing the Mass read in English. He felt betrayed by a religion that abruptly switched positions on such matters as diet and traditional dress for nuns. Because he still required rigidity in religion, he looked for a church that was as conservative as he was — and found the Mormons.

"I've always had a love of music, and through the Mormon Tabernacle Choir I became acquainted with the Mormon Church. I liked their belief that America was a divine nation. I had always believed that we had a special place in helping to solve the problems of the world. At the same time, even though I was still deep in the closet, I wanted a church that would make it easier for me to accept my homosexuality.

"So I asked one of the Mormon missionaries what the church's position on homosexuality was. He obviously didn't know what he was talking about, for he indicated that they were very liberal. For me, this was perfect. By becoming a Mormon I could join a conservative church with liberal views on sexuality. In the South China Sea, therefore, I was baptised a Mormon, and within three years I became an elder, the highest position you can become.

"It was quite some time before I discovered the true Mormon attitude toward homosexuality, and even then I wasn't ready to deal with it. You see, I tended to buy religion, *when* I bought it, hook, line, and sinker."

Whether in or out of church services, Matlovich had "a really good time" in Da Nang because for once he wasn't in love with anyone and didn't get hurt — at least not physically. Unfortunately, with only two weeks left of his second tour of duty in Vietnam, he volunteered for a special mission to clear an area that had been mined and nearly met the destiny he subconsciously desired.

"I remember it as vivid as can be. We were shoveling, looking for mines. It was really hot, so I decided to take a break. I walked about twenty feet away from everyone else, and I stuck my shovel in the ground, but it wouldn't stand up. So I gave it a harder push, and it blew up. I saw it happen. I saw the explosion go right up past me. The next thing I knew, I was lying on the ground. I immediately checked myself to see if I was all there. I could see, but my right lung was blown down into my stomach, and I bled internally. I had holes all over me where the shrapnel went in. I was in tremendous pain, but I wasn't knocked unconscious. Then I was taken to the hospital."

Matlovich stayed in the hospital for four months. Although he was in great pain much of the time, the physical pain was nothing compared to the emotional trauma he lived with; he found shrapnel preferable to the guilt and shame he suffered as a closeted homosexual. His hospital stay, therefore, was in comparison a restful, peaceful experience. It allowed him the opportunity to forget about internal battles for a while and to concentrate on getting well instead.

After four months in the hospital in Vietnam, Leonard was sent to hopitals in Japan and the United States. Then he recuperated at home with his family. While there, he began to consider his next assignment in the Air Force, and he consulted the Air Force's "magic book" on career fields. The first thing to strike his eye was the chapter on "Photogrametric Cartographic Analysis" — map-making. Enraptured by visions of going up the Amazon and exploring uncharted regions of the world, he enrolled in the Photogrametric Cartographic Tech School at Fort Belvoir, near Alexandria, Virginia. Following graduation in early 1970, he was stationed at March Air Force Base in Riverside, California.

At March, Matlovich spent his time making T-10 plates —

graphic designs which enabled pilots to sit in simulators and practice bombing runs over Moscow without ever having to leave the ground. When they looked through the windows of the simulator, the pilots saw exactly what they would see if they were actually flying over Russia. While this may have been exciting for the pilots, it was terribly boring for Leonard. The last thing on earth he wanted was a desk job, and making T-10 plates was just that.

To make matters worse, Leonard found himself increasingly alienated from others because of his repressed sexuality yet increasingly desperate to conceal it. He would go to great lengths to establish cover for himself. As a staff sergeant in charge of the barracks there, he often joined in the general mistreatment of anyone suspected to be gay. Once, when a young airman was caught with a gay skin magazine, Matlovich ridiculed him, along with the others. But every time he made fun of someone or told a queer joke, he "died a little bit on the inside," because he knew that his behavior was simply the result of cowardice and self-loathing.

To escape the boredom of his job and the increasing trauma of self-disgust, Leonard became even more deeply involved with the Mormon Church.

"For about a year it was a very important part of my life. I went to services all the time, every Sunday and Wednesday. I also became involved in study groups and volunteer activities. Mostly I was involved with youth groups, going hiking and camping up in the mountains with the kids and things like that. Involvement with the church is a total commitment, a whole lifestyle, like a cult, because once they get you, they try to control every aspect of your life. And I was certainly willing to give my all — for a while.

"I also advanced rapidly in the church. One of the things Mormons believe is eternal progression. You're here to become one with God. So part of being a Mormon is becoming a priest for the church. You go through interviews and meet certain requirements to move up the ladder. Because I didn't have much to do at March, I fulfilled those requirements very fast.

"In some ways, the church gave me comfort. But it wasn't

healthy, for it was really just a crutch, a place to escape. When I first heard the church's official doctrine on homosexuality — when I learned that what I had been told at the beginning about homosexuality wasn't true at all — then it all began to unravel for me. I began to suspect that I was being sold a false bill of goods. I still wasn't out of the closet yet — far from it — but I was experiencing a lot of turmoil, and the church, rather than help me relieve that turmoil, simply added to it."

Exasperated with his job at March and with his life in general, Matlovich volunteered for a third tour of duty in Vietnam and returned to Da Nang in July 1970, less than one year after stepping on the mine. This time he saw no combat duty. Instead, he worked in the military's "Vietnamization" program, teaching the South Vietnamese to take over in preparation for America's eventual withdrawal from the country. His job was to supervise the training of civil engineers — electricians, plumbers, carpenters, and the like. He also was responsible for keeping records. In some ways it was an easy life, living in an air-conditioned barracks and working with his own personal Vietnamese interpreter. And because he was involved in on-site supervision, it was also a satisfying one.

If this kind of life was not particularly exciting for Leonard, neither was it predictable or uneventful, especially on a personal level. Despite past hurts, he kept trying to reach out to other people. One of those was a man named Clark.

"We became good friends, and I cultivated that friendship. He was the first person I ever told I was gay. I don't remember how we got to this point, but he wanted to know if I was homosexual or not. Since we couldn't say the word out loud, we arranged that he would write the question and leave it in my top desk drawer. I would then answer yes or no. Well, when I opened the drawer, I found what I expected to find: the question, 'Are you a homosexual?' I answered yes. After that, our friendship kind of collapsed. I thought he was probably gay too, but because he was engaged, I never considered asking him the same question. He moved to a different part of the base, and we just didn't see each other as often as before. "There was also this kid named Ralph, who I am convinced was gay. We used to wrestle a lot. He would pick me up by the crotch of my pants and shake me upside down; we were just horsing around. He even moved in my hootch one night. But older people complained about a younger sergeant having such nice quarters, so he moved out the next day. I'm convinced that if he had not moved out, we would have had a relationship."

It was in Da Nang that Matlovich received his second medal — the Purple Heart. It was awarded to him in recognition of the wounds he suffered the year before. He accepted it with characteristic grace, modesty, and humor. "If you got a scratch, you got a Purple Heart," he told friends. "I know people who got Purple Hearts when barbed wire cut them." Still, because he paid dearly for it, he cherished the medal. In time, however, he would receive awards he valued far more.

In July 1971, Matlovich's third tour of duty came to an end, and he left Vietnam — this time for good

3

The Awakening

At the end of Matlovich's third tour of duty in Vietnam, it was once again time for him to consider his next assignment. He reconsulted the Air Force's manual on career options and ran across a program called "Special Forces" at Hurlburt Field, Eglin Air Force Base, Ft. Walton Beach, Florida. Thinking this must have something to do with fighting Communists in the jungles of yet another foreign country or something equally adventurous, Leonard volunteered for the program and was accepted, only to find himself the head of the electric shop on the base. After Vietnam, it was stultifying to sit in an office most of the day pushing paper, and he quickly began looking for an alternative.

He found it through the Air Force's Drug and Alcohol Abuse program at Hurlburt.

"In Vietnam we had two major problems — drug abuse and race relations. Because of the war, both had reached critical proportions, and the military had decided to do something about them by establishing drug and alcohol abuse and race relations programs. I decided to volunteer to become a drug and alcohol abuse counselor, since I felt that was the more pressing problem. So I volunteered and was accepted into the counseling program at Hurlburt Field. That was the beginning of a real change in my life. In some ways it was an odd choice, for I had never used an illegal drug in my entire life, never. I didn't even know that there were such things as marijuana brownies until I went to a party one night and someone tried to give me one. Because my friends all knew this, there was never a time when my friends didn't try to get me drunk or stoned. It came to be a challenge for them.

"I was so adamant about not using drugs or alcohol mainly because I was afraid I had an alcoholic personality. When I was young, my kidneys didn't function right, and the doctor told my mother that beer would help them to function better. So I was raised on beer as a kid, and I grew up loving it. Unfortunately, two of my uncles who I love very much were alcoholics. I saw what alcohol did to them, and that had an effect on me.

"Nevertheless, I did get drunk a few times. As a young airman, when I turned twenty-one and could legally drink, I went out and got so plastered on beer that I slipped and fell on my own vomit. I've never been able to drink beer since. After that, I switched to mixed drinks, but I went out and did the same thing again. Then in Vietnam I got so drunk that I couldn't get out of bed during an attack one night, even though rockets were exploding all around me. That's when I said, 'No more.' I quit drinking in 1968.

"Fortunately, I have never had any moral qualms about drugs or drinking. I think you have a right to do with your body what you want to do. My icebox today is full of alcohol for friends, but I don't use it. I don't even see it."

After graduating from the counseling school, Matlovich served as a drug and alcohol abuse counselor for a year. He met with three or four clients a day, trying to help them overcome their addictions. He was a sympathetic and impartial listener, but he could be tough if he felt it was in the client's best interests. One of his clients, for instance, was a "constant whiner" who often talked about suicide. Finally, one day Matlovich told him how to do it and encouraged him to try if he thought it would make his life any easier. According to Leonard, it was exactly what the client needed. He didn't kill himself — and he never whined again.

Although he believed he was a good counselor, helping some people to turn their lives around, Matlovich still wasn't completely satisfied. By chance, one day he had nothing to do and dropped by to observe a race relations class. He instantly felt at home there. Determined to become a race relations instructor, he returned to school again and submitted to a battery of sensitivity training workshops. Thus began the period which he later described as the happiest four years of his life.

"The school was an experience I'll never forget. At the time, I was trying to overcome my racism, but I still didn't believe in the necessity of the '64 Civil Rights Act, and occasionally I used words like 'nigger' or 'jigaboo' or 'pickaninny.' But every time I did I think my heart stopped. I knew by then that it was wrong. The experiences I had in Vietnam and the contact I had with black people there convinced me that racism just didn't make any sense.

"In Vietnam I constantly met blacks who demonstrated that they were just like everyone else, yet they weren't being given the same rights. Here we were sending Americans of all colors to Vietnam to fight for democracy, and in Pensacola, Florida, when a black American soldier was brought home in a casket, his body was refused burial in a white cemetery. I recognized the unfairness of this double standard, but I still had a long way to go before I was capable of treating blacks as equals on a personal level.

"One of the exercises at the school that helped me to overcome my racism was called 'Primitive to Dinner.' First, we put a sheet on the floor, and in the middle we placed an unsliced loaf of bread, a half gallon of milk, and a whole chicken. Then we sat down to eat. But we couldn't use utensils; we had to use our hands. And we couldn't feed ourselves; we had to feed the person to our right. Well, one thing my mother always taught me was never to drink after anyone from the same glass, and as I watched this half gallon of milk coming around the room toward me, I could feel myself getting more and more nauseous. These people were violating everything I had grown up believing. Not only did they want me to share my food on such an intimate level, but they wanted me to do it with black people! Somehow I managed to get through the experience, but it had quite an effect on me. It really made me take a deeper look at myself and the values I held. It was something I needed — even if to this day I still don't drink after people."

Emerging from the school with a deeper understanding of minority groups and a greater feeling for their experiences as second-class citizens in the United States, Leonard began teaching his own race relations class. It was, in his own estimation, "one of the most unique race relations classes in the military," and he became, by all accounts, an outstanding instructor. He did this by making use of innovative techniques and an outrageous manner. In the process, he exposed his students to ideas which were new and startling to them.

Matlovich's favorite classroom method was role-playing. In one exercise, he instructed the minority members of the class (usually about one-fourth of the total) to bid for ownership of the others. Each minority member would own three or four white males. The minorities would then set the classroom rules — if and when their "slaves" could go to lunch, take a break, smoke, or whatever. Matlovich gave them complete control. He was astonished to see how quickly people began to adopt alternative points of view.

Another technique he used was to give history lectures but to reverse the data. Leafing through old textbooks, he found scores of ridiculous racial theories which he subverted. For instance, one theory he taught was the "pepper seed theory." Matlovich told his students that the greatest scientists in the world took the skulls of a white man and a black man and filled each full of pepper seeds. Because more seeds fit into the skull of the black man, then clearly the black man was more intelligent. Leonard later confessed that in the actual historical experiment the findings were the opposite, and for years the U.S. Army used this as scientific proof that whites were more intelligent than blacks.

Leonard used other methods as well. He told his students about a law that had once been enacted in New York City forbidding blacks from being firefighters because their noses were too large and they would inhale too much smoke. He quoted from

Malcolm X that the white man was the devil. "Remove the D," he said, "and he's evil." If a newspaper article appeared about a black woman killing her child, Matlovich pointed out that she was probably half-white, and it was the white blood in her that made her do it. While many of his students considered his teaching methods outrageous, Leonard was determined to shock his students' sensibilities however he could in order to bring about change.

At the end of each course, Leonard routinely showed the film, *The Eye of the Storm*, a CBS special concerning the experiments of a teacher in Iowa who divided her students into two groups, children with blue eyes and those with brown eyes. In the experiment, one group was given special privileges that were denied to the other, including the right to make rules governing behavior. Notions of equality and fairness were temporarily abandoned by the group in power, causing the subjugated group to agitate for justice. As a result, the children learned a great deal about prejudice and racism. For Leonard, the film summed up exactly what he was trying to teach; his own students, he said, were invariably moved by the film

Matlovich's students were not the only ones to be affected by his class. Through teaching, Leonard himself changed. He finally overcame his racism. He also became — as far as racial matters were concerned — what he called a starry-eyed liberal. ("That's a person who has his feet planted firmly in the air. Of course, I didn't know then that to have one's feet in the air would one day be a virtue and not a vice.") Furthermore, teaching brought him an increasing sense of his own self-worth — and for the first time ever, Leonard began to sense a way to deal with a problem that was of even greater concern to him than race relations — his homsexuality. He knew he had to do something about his sexuality, for his personal life was becoming increasingly distressing. The longer he postponed dealing with it, the more difficult the problem became. When he fell in love with his roommate, a man named Tim, while still a drug and alcohol abuse counselor, he realized he had finally reached a turning point. Either he had to confront his internal battle directly or face a lifetime of continual rejection and increasing isolation.

"When I met Tim, I was still looking for love but always barking up the wrong tree. With Tim, I thought I had at last found love, for he did things that led me to believe it. One time, for instance, I was supposed to have been home at a certain time and didn't come back, and he overreacted to that. He said, 'I was worried about you. Where were you? You were suppposed to be home. I had all these plans.' And I thought, 'Wow, that's not a normal reaction for one man to have for another. How wonderful.'

"Another time, a friend of Tim's came over. Tim was lying on the couch, the friend was at the other end of the couch, and I was sitting in a chair. Tim had a Coke bottle in his mouth. While he was staring at his friend, he kept putting the Coke bottle in and out of his mouth, and I thought, 'My God, what's going on here?'

"And one time before Tim went to bed I gave him a rub-down. The next time I tried to do it he absolutely refused because he said it gave him horrible nightmares. I fantasized about what these nightmares were. I hoped they were 'nightmares' of the two of us making love.

"Because of all these things, I was convinced that Tim, like my friend Clark in Vietnam, was gay, even if he didn't know it yet. And because I couldn't continue to live with him under the circumstances, feeling the way I did, I finally broke down and told Tim I was gay, thinking he might say the same or at least offer positive reinforcement. Instead, five minutes later, he packed up and moved out.

"This was incredibly devastating to me. It ripped me to pieces on the inside and made me feel incredibly dirty, so dirty that it was almost impossible to shave in the morning. I thought, 'My God, if this is the way everyone reacts when he finds out I'm gay, what good is life?' It was pretty sad, actually, for here I was, a drug and alcohol abuse counselor, and I was in desperate need of counseling myself.

"Life seemed so bleak at that moment that I went in the closet and got a shotgun. Then I went in Tim's room, lay down on his bed, and cried and cried, saying to myself, 'Why, God? Why me? What did I do to deserve this? Why can't I find love?

Why can't I find someone to hold?' It was a terrible thing to be nearly thirty years old and never to have held anyone other than family.

"Taking the shells out, I put the shotgun to my head and pulled the trigger. I was going to put the shells back in and do the same, for I couldn't see any way out. I thought it was the end of the line. Luckily, though, I had a dog named Ralph, and all Ralph ever asked for or gave was love. I thought of him, put the gun down, and the two of us went for a walk in the woods, where I just cried some more. When I came home, I called a friend of mine, a former high school roommate in England who was a psychiatrist, and told him what had happened. He helped me to get through this crisis.

"It took a few days, naturally, to pull myself together, but thanks to my training as a counselor, I was able to do it. However, it took years to get over it fully. As a matter of fact, I used to drive by the house of Tim's parents in Mobile, Alabama, where he went on the weekends, just to sit in the car and look for him. I saw him a number of times, but I never did anything about it. I just sat and watched."

At about the same time, the Air Force sent Matlovich to New Orleans for a drug conference, and he made his first attempt to enter a gay bar. Trailing a drag queen down Bourbon Street, he followed her into a bar called the Cavern. As soon as he walked in the front door, however, he heard someone mutter, "Vice Squad." Whether the speaker was referring to him or to someone else, Leonard did not know. He responded by instantly turning around and walking back out — and he didn't enter another gay bar for years. If someone hadn't said that, he later recalled, he might have come out a lot earlier. But just hearing those words terrified him and caused him to put an extra couple of locks on his closet door.

Despite these setbacks, Matlovich eventually summoned the courage a year later to talk about homosexuality in one of his race relations classes. Inspired by a television documentary which mentioned homosexuals as victims of prejudice, at the very end of class one day he asked the question, "What is the most discriminated-against group of people in America today?"

When his students suggested blacks, Latinos, and American Indians, he walked to the blackboard and wrote, "Homosexuals." He felt it was something he had to do, and not just for personal reasons. The response was so positive that he soon incorporated it as a regular feature of his class.

Expanding his theme, Leonard even went so far as to bring in an investigator from the Air Force's Office of Special Investigations (OSI) to explain why the military didn't admit homosexuals. He began to look for news of homosexuals in the newspapers, and he read all he could find on the subject in books. Since Leonard had never met an openly gay person in his life, he knew little more than his students did, but he did his best to keep ahead. For three years his students discussed homosexuality in his classes, and all that time Matlovich himself was still in the closet.

In the course of his research, Matlovich ran across an article in the *Air Force Times* entitled, "Homosexuals in Uniform." The article mentioned Dr. Frank Kameny, a prominent gay activist who was the founder of the Washington, D.C. branch of the Mattachine Society, one of the first gay organizations in the country, in 1961. Seeking further information, Leonard called Kameny in Washington on the phone one night and told him about his race relations class. In turn, the activist told the Air Force sergeant about his efforts to help defend gay people who had been dishonorably discharged from the military. Leonard, who knew nothing about all this, was amazed. He talked to Kameny on the phone for about an hour, and at the end of the conversation, having heard Kameny refer to "the ideal case" several times, Leonard asked exactly what he meant by this.

Kameny responded that he and a group of military lawyers at the ACLU, in an attempt to challenge military policy excluding homosexuals, were seeking a career individual with a perfect military record who wanted to remain in the military but who was willing to say — in court, if necessary — that he or she was gay. That described Matlovich perfectly — all except the last part — so he told Kameny that he had someone in mind who might consider volunteering as the test case guinea pig. He didn't talk to Kameny again for another year. In the meantime, he had a lot of exploring to do.

One day when the subject of homosexuality was being discussed in Matlovich's class, a friend in the class mentioned that he and his wife had dropped by a restaurant called the Yum Yum in Pensacola, forty miles away. The food was wonderful, he said, but when the floor show started, he was shocked to discover that the staff and clientele were gay. Suddenly, fourteen-year-old boys wearing nothing but jockstraps appeared to serve cocktails, and when the man got up to use the restroom, a huge crowd followed him inside to watch. Leonard was sceptical of his friend's story, but since he had always been terrified to enter the Yum Yum, which he had heard about before, he had no way of knowing if the story was true. Therefore, he decided to investigate — all in the line of duty, of course.

"At the time I had a three-quarter ton truck with snow tires. I drove it to Pensacola but parked over three blocks away because I was afraid that someone would see it and be able to identify me. Then I walked to the bar, hoping the entire way that my friend had lied about what he had seen. I didn't want those things to be true. I wanted people to be like me.

"I walked in the door and made it two steps down the hallway before I ran out because I was afraid. Then I turned around and walked three steps before I ran out again. Finally I walked four steps and turned the corner into the bar. I was relieved to see that there were no fourteen-year-old boys in there. Furthermore, the bathroom was so small that one person could hardly get in, much less an entire crowd. Instead, the place was filled with grown men and women who were laughing and smiling, and I said, 'I'm in paradise. This is incredible.'

"About a million pounds must have come off my shoulders that night. For the next three months, I went there every Friday and Saturday night. I never talked to anyone, but I watched and observed, because it was part of my race relations class and I was learning. Unfortunately, one of the things I learned was that I might have to leave the Air Force. Back then, the OSI used to look for military personnel in gay bars so they could throw them out in disgrace. I didn't want to be in constant fear of losing my job. I wanted to be a happy person like all these other people around me. So I began to think about taking a civilian job instead.

"One night I finally sat down at the bar and started talking to a woman who was a bank president. She confessed to me that she had the same fears I did about losing her job if her superiors found out she was a lesbian. Suddenly, I felt all this weight coming back onto my shoulders again. It was terrible. Then I thought, 'Why should I get out of the military and lose a job that I love so much only to get involved in something I really don't care about and still have the same fears?' That's when I decided that some day, somehow, I was going to fight this stupidity. I didn't know when or where or how I was going to do it, but I knew I had to do it. I knew I had to make a commitment to fight ignorance."

Three months after Matlovich entered the Yum Yum for the first time, he finally met someone he could wrap his arms around — and then some. The man's name was Bob, and he was a fellow serviceman. He and Leonard got along so well that Leonard invited him to dinner at his place. After dinner it happened.

"I was washing dishes when I turned around, and all of a sudden we found ourselves in each other's arms, holding each other. It was almost like a movie script. Then we went into the bedroom, and I just shook and shook. After thirty years, there was a void in my life that was finally being filled. It was wonderful, finally getting rid of all the anxiety of so many years."

Leonard and Bob met sexually only once after that, but Leonard didn't mind. He didn't find love, but he did find a way to approximate the feeling. Besides, Bob was, if anything, even more closeted than Leonard. Rather than risk being seen at a gay bar in Pensacola by people he knew, Bob used to drive all the way to New Orleans to experience gay life. Leonard, who was seeking a way out of the closet, not a path further in, had no desire to follow Bob's example.

One of his first tentative steps out of the closet, besides visiting gay bars and meeting other gay people, was to quit the Mormon Church.

"Once I started teaching race relations, I really had no room for the church any more. Besides, I was beginning to realize that

I was a good person despite, and perhaps because of, my homosexuality. It was a simple process, really. I just applied what I taught in the classroom to my own situation. If being black was just as beautiful as being white, then why shouldn't being gay be just as beautiful as being straight? If, after experiencing years of prejudice and oppression, blacks were no longer willing to sit at the back of the bus, why should I?

"I finally realized that it was okay for me to be gay. I might not ever have realized this without the help of my black friends, students, and co-workers. That's why I say that everything I am today or ever hope to be I owe to black Americans.

"The funny thing about freedom is that when you finally allow yourself to experience it, you can't give it up — no matter who tells you that you should. Words like truth and justice mean something once more, and you develop your own ideas, your own private morality. When you do this, you are no longer at the mercy of those who would oppress you. Suddenly, things become very clear, and you know when someone is selling you a false bill of goods.

"Consequently, when I finally accepted myself for what I was, I knew that the Mormon Church and I couldn't both be right when it came to homosexuality. Since I was right, they were wrong; there was no longer any question about it. And because I'm a person of such strong convictions, I decided to sever my connection with the church all at once. So I stopped going to services. They reached out with their tentacles, trying to hold me back, and when they failed, they considered me a fallen sheep. I considered myself a victor, however, for I was at last coming to grips with a situation that had long needed addressing.

"Leaving the church was very significant for me, for it marked the end of religion in my life. It was the last hurrah. I wasn't officially excommunicated for another year, not until they found out exactly who I was and what I believed — which I didn't even know when I quit. But by the time they excommunicated me, I didn't care. The whole thing was more like a comic opera than anything else."

Shortly after this, in recognition of his outstanding success in Florida, Matlovich was transferred to Langley Air Force Base in Hampton, Virginia, where the national race relations program was headquartered. His new assignment took him all over the United States to evaluate various race relations programs at individual bases and to try to elevate them to his standards. Between cross-country trips, he visited gay bars in nearby Norfolk, where the local high school students chanted, "We don't smoke, We don't drink, Nor folk, Nor folk!" Of the two gay bars in town, the first he visited, Mickey's, was a dive. The other, however, was "fabulous." It was a giant dance bar called the Cue, and there Leonard continued to explore the gay life he was beginning to enjoy.

He did not forget about his telephone conversation with Frank Kameny a year earlier, however. Since he was now stationed so close to Kameny's home in Washington, D.C., he called Kameny once again and suggested a meeting. At that meeting, in July 1974, he confessed to Kameny that he was the "friend" he had mentioned before and informed him that he was considering fighting the Air Force on the homosexual issue. If Kameny agreed, he added, he was willing to be the test case they had talked about. It was the end result of a long process of self-discovery and his own rather extraordinary way of putting the years of guilt and shame behind him.

"I did it because I had to. I knew that the military would throw me out if they knew I was gay, even though I had a perfect military record with numerous awards and medals. That didn't make sense to me. For four years I had talked about equality and justice in the classroom, and at last I had begun to believe in it.

"Of course, I was terrified of the consequences. I was particularly afraid that I'd never see my parents again, because I didn't think they would be able to accept it. I thought I'd lose everything. But I knew that whatever I stood to lose was no more important than what I was gaining — my own self-image, my own honor. In the end, I had no choice."

After meeting with Matlovich and reviewing his record, Kameny decided that here indeed was the perfect test case he had been seeking. He introduced Leonard to an attorney working with the ACLU on military issues, David Addlestone, and the three began meeting regularly to plan strategy. At those meetings, Kameny and his lawyer did everything they could to talk Matlovich out of his decision because they wanted to make sure that he was committed — a technique Leonard approved. He, too, wanted to be sure he had no second thoughts. He had invested twelve years of his life in the Air Force, after all, and once his superiors learned that he was gay, his career would, in all likelihood, be finished.

With strategy set, the only thing remaining was for Leonard to summon the necessary courage to go through with his plans. That took about a year. Ironically, the incident that spurred him to action at last was one involving his dogs — his mutt, Ralph, and his Siberian husky, Samantha. Previously, when he had traveled around the country on business, the Air Force sent him for only three or four days at the most, which was the longest he was willing to leave his dogs at the pound. But when the Air Force changed that policy and proposed sending him on the road for several weeks at a time, Leonard balked. He had to think of some way to resolve the situation

His solution was simple. If he told the Air Force that he was gay, then he knew he wouldn't be going anywhere. Rather than put his dogs in the pound for two weeks, therefore, he drove to Washington to pick up the letter that he and his lawyer had drafted informing the Air Force that he was gay. For Matlovich, it was a logical reaction: his dogs were all that he had when it came to love.

But not for long.

4

The Battle Begins

When Matlovich met Frank Kameny, the gay activist was directing his energies down a variety of avenues, including public lecturing, legal referrals, and political organizing. According to Kameny

"When I founded the gay movement in Washington in 1961, nobody had done anything, and nothing was getting done, so we had a blank slate on which to write our agenda. Although we recognized that getting into politics was very important, after a good bit of casting around we decided that ultimately the area in which we wanted to concentrate was what we called 'Gays v. the Government.' That involved specifically the three areas of civil service employment, security clearances, and the armed services.

"Within the armed services, we pursued a mixed bag of cases for years — with relatively little success. But when I met Leonard, I knew that his case was different. I had had other cases of gay people in the service who wanted to declare and get out or who were attacked by the military and wanted to defend themselves, but he was the first who came foward, wanted to stay in, and wanted to attack just that way. He took the initiative. He threw down the gauntlet and said, in effect, 'You are wrong, I am right, and it's time you change your policy.'

"Consequently, the case was ours from the outset. It was created specifically the way some of the civil rights cases had been created in the fifties and sixties — to change a particular situation. And like the early civil rights cases, we took the opposition by surprise. The military really wasn't quite prepared for any kind of resistance on this question. At that time their regulations were a mess. They certainly weren't prepared for a case like Leonard's, which was a perfect case on the merits. He was a fine candidate to make this challenge."

David Addlestone, the lawyer from the ACLU's Military Rights Project who was introduced to Matlovich by Kameny, also agreed that Leonard was "the perfect client."

"He hadn't done anything yet, he hadn't told anybody about his intentions, he had an absolutely incredible record, and he was coming at it from a very All-American, apple-pie approach, rather than a left-wing, 'militant gay activist' approach. Furthermore, he was extremely cooperative. All systems just sort of clicked. It seemed to me the case was going to fly."

Because Addlestone had been a Judge Advocate in the Air Force with previous experience defending individuals accused of homosexual acts, he was in a good position to advise Leonard on how to proceed with his case. With Kameny, who stepped back into an informal consultant role, Addlestone, partner Susan Hewman, and Matlovich began to plan strategy in mid-1974.

One of the first things Addlestone did was to acquaint Matlovich with current Air Force regulations concerning homosexuality. According to AFM 39-12, Chapter 2, Section H, Paragraph 2-103:

"Homosexuality is not tolerated in the Air Force. Participation in a homosexual act, or proposing or attempting to do so, is considered serious misbehavior regardless of whether the role of a person in a particular act was active or passive. Similarly, airmen who have homosexual tendencies, or who associate habitually with persons known to them to be homosexuals, do not meet Air Force standards."

None of this was new or surprising to Matlovich. What he did not know, however, was that AFM 39-12 contained an "exception rule" which Addlestone proposed might be applied to him:

"It is the general policy to discharge members of the Air Force who fall within the purview of this section. Exceptions to permit retention may be authorized only where the most unusual circumstances exist and provided the airman's ability to perform military service has not been compromised." Unfortunately, AFM 39-12 did not specify exactly what those "unusual circumstances" might be, other than to note that intoxication "in itself" is no excuse, although it "may be extenuating in a given case." Furthermore, "an exception is not warranted simply because the airman has extensive service, since such person is expected to set an example of high moral standards." Only in one case did 39-12 provide a concrete example of what might constitute an exception:

"An exception may be considered in a case involving participation prior to entry in the Air Force provided it is established that youthful curiosity was involved, that there is no current pattern of homosexuality, and that the airman's ability to perform military service has not been compromised."

In other words, being drunk was no excuse (although it could be), while being young *was* one, as long as the transgression had been acknowledged and foresworn. It was no wonder Kameny called the regulations a mess.

Because Matlovich's service record was so impressive, Addlestone argued that they take advantage of this exception rule by claiming that his record alone constituted the "unusual circumstance" which might keep him in the Air Force. At the same time, Addlestone recognized that if Matlovich *did* qualify for retention under the rule, their major goal — to make it possible for *all* homosexuals to serve in the military, regardless of their particular circumstances — would remain unfulfilled. This led to certain difficulties for Leonard, for he wanted to right what he considered to be a great wrong, and moral victories are not won by qualifying for exceptions to the regulations.

Therefore, Addlestone proposed challenging the Air Force on constitutional grounds as well. He would argue, when the time came, that AFM 39-12 violated Matlovich's right to privacy, due process, and equal protection under the laws guaranteed by the First, Fifth, and Ninth Amendments to the Constitution. The assault on the Air Force would therefore be led on two fronts, and if the case faltered on one front, Addlestone would carry on with the other. Because the Air Force was unlikely to accept either argument, both could be taken on to the civil courts — all the way to the Supreme Court, if necessary.

With tactics set, Addlestone, Hewman, Kameny, and Matlovich still had to decide the best way for Leonard to fire the opening salvo. According to Addlestone:

"There were several ways we could have done it. Matt was getting ready to accept an award for being super-soldier, and I said, 'If you really want to go blasting out with this, you could thank the general and kiss him on both cheeks on the parade ground.' Frank [Kameny] sort of liked that idea at first. He's really into media events. But Matt and I were more comfortable with playing it close to the chest. So I said, 'Let's approach it in a non-public fashion first to see what's going to happen.' Well, we knew what was going to happen — they wouldn't want him once they knew what his sexual preference was — but we wanted to play it this way first."

They decided the best way for Matlovich to let the Air Force know his intentions was simply to write a letter through the chain of command to the Secretary of the Air Force, which he would deliver to his immediate superior officer at Langley, Captain Dennis M. Collins. The letter, dated March 6, 1975, was brief and concise:

"After some years of uncertainty, I have arrived at the conclusion that my sexual preferences are homosexual as opposed to heterosexual. I have also concluded that my sexual preferences will in no way interfere with my Air Force duties, as my preferences are now open. It is therefore requested that those provisions in AFM 39-12 relating to the discharge of homosexuals be waived in my case. . . . In sum, I consider myself to be a homosexual and fully qualified for further military service. My almost twelve years of unblemished service supports this position."

Leonard was understandably nervous when he delivered his letter that clear March day:

"You have to understand that I had twelve years of my life invested in the military, and once the letter left my hand, my career was finished. I walked into the office anyway, and my boss was standing behind his desk. I said, 'Captain Collins, I have a letter I'd like for you to read. I think you ought to sit down before you read it.' He said, 'No, I'll stand.' I said, 'Really, Captain Collins, I think you ought to sit down.' He continued to stand, though, so I gave him the letter. He read it and immediately sat down. He kind of just slumped in his chair. Then he looked at me and asked, 'What does this mean?' And I said, 'This means *Brown v. the Board of Education.'* Since he was black, I knew he would understand. I added, 'We as lesbians and gays aren't going to take the discrimination any more.' Then I left the office. Two seconds later, I found myself a military lawyer.

"I was very lucky to get the military lawyer I got, Captain Larson Jaenicke. He was very good. It was just fate, for I accepted the first lawyer I was assigned. When he first read the letter I gave to Captain Collins, he thought that I wanted to get out of the Air Force. He said, 'This is dumb. Why did you do this? You should have come and talked to me first.' I said, 'I don't think you understand. Read the letter again.' He read it again, and broke into a big smile. Then he said, 'Oh, now I understand what's going on. This is wonderful.' He was excited because he sympathized with me and knew this was going to be a challenging case. So I gave him David Addlestone's phone number in Washington, D.C., and they got in touch."

Later that day, Matlovich notified one other person of his intentions. This was a far more difficult disclosure than the other two had been, for it required a confession that he had dreaded for years. He phoned home.

"After about forty-five minutes of stammering, I somehow managed to tell my mother not only that I was gay but also that I was challenging the Air Force's ban on homosexuality. She responded as a stereotypical Catholic mother. She said that God was punishing her and that's why I was that way. Then she said that I hadn't prayed enough or seen enough psychiatrists. I told her I had calluses all over my knees from praying. Finally she said that my father would blame it all on her and throw her out of the house as a result. She was convinced that he could not handle it. 'I've been married to him for years,' she said, 'and I know him better than you.' So I decided not to tell my father because I didn't want my mother to be thrown out. She was really very afraid of that."

According to Michael Bedwell, who met Leonard a few months after this and was to become a lifelong friend:

"When Leonard came out, his mother was hurt, shocked, and angry. She said to him, 'How could you do this to us? Don't tell your father.' Her reaction was an extremely emotional one — but so was their entire relationship. Leonard was always sending her presents: orchids, porcelain figures, dolls, even television sets. Nevertheless, he argued with her frequently. I've been with him when they've had an argument over the phone which led to three or four more phone calls in succession. Leonard would say, 'Mother, stop calling, leave me alone, you're driving me crazy, everything's fine, good-bye.' Ten minutes later, the phone would ring again. She'd be crying, and he'd say something like, 'Well, are you sure you're all right?' The important thing, though, is that they loved each other, and that was what it was all about."

The Air Force's response was quite different from that of Leonard's mother. Initially confused, it was soon cold, calculating, and underhanded. For several weeks, Matlovich's superiors allowed him to fulfill his duties in the Race Relations Program while they decided what to do. Then his duties changed, and he became little more than an office clerk and errand boy. Eventually, claims Matlovich, he was fired because the Air Force felt that his presence in the military would cause collapse of morale and discipline among the young troops.

Ironically, their next step was to put him in charge of a barracks full of young airmen. Matlovich suspected he was being set up. His suspicions were confirmed when he was requested to accompany the first sergeant on barracks inspections. Against Air Force policy, the first sergeant conducted the inspections during off-duty hours, rousing the airmen from their beds, where they slept in shorts or in the nude. Leonard believed that they were hoping to catch him staring at the naked airmen, which they could introduce as evidence at an administrative discharge hearing.

This was not the only devious way in which the Air Force

dealt with Matlovich. His superiors also scheduled interviews with the Office of Special Investigations without letting him know until minutes beforehand, and some of these they scheduled when they knew his lawyer could not attend. Fortunately, his military counsel, Captain Jaenicke, was well acquainted with these kinds of maneuvers and was able to help Leonard on a number of occasions with warnings about how the Air Force was likely to entrap him. Jaenicke's advice was for Leonard to provide as little information as possible, giving them only his name, rank, and serial number whenever he was questioned. Sometimes the pressure the Air Force applied to get Matlovich to drop the case was intense.

"Once, they said to me, 'We don't believe you really are a homosexual. We believe you're doing this just because you're a race relations instructor and you're fighting for minority rights. We'll forget all about it if you sign a statement saying that.' I just gave them my name, rank, and serial number. This happened over and over again, and I never budged.

"To relieve the pressure and to make a point, Jaenicke tried to turn the tables on them when he could. The base commander, Lieutenant Colonel Schofield, called Jaenicke into his office once to ask him about my conduct as an individual. Instead of replying, Jaenicke asked him if he thought homosexuals should serve in the military as a matter of principle. Col. Schofield, who used to give nude swimming parties at his home, answered, 'Under no conditions should that be allowed.' When Jaenicke asked, 'Well, what about people who give nude swimming parties?' Schofield replied, 'That's not fair. What I do in the privacy of my house is my business.' Jaenicke concluded, 'Thank you, Colonel. That's what this case is all about.'"

Dealing with Air Force pressure was one thing; dealing with the reactions of friends and co-workers was another. Few of Matlovich's gay friends outside the military supported his decision to confront the Air Force. Many tried to talk him out of it. To protect the gay people he knew in the military, Leonard deliberately isolated himself for several months before he sent his letter. His efforts went unappreciated. Later, when word of his disclosure spread across the base, other gay people treated him "like the plague." Some even ran to the other side of the building when they saw him in the post exchange. They were afraid that if they associated with Leonard, the Office of Special Investigations would interrogate them too. Their fears were not unfounded. In the course of its investigations, the OSI called in many of Matlovich's former co-workers, roommates, and acquaintances, gay and straight, to collect information for use against him.

The nature of those investigations could be brutal, as Leonard soon found out for himself. According to Addlestone:

"They called him in and wanted to ask him questions, questions I felt they had a right to ask based on my reading of the case law. Some of these were intrusive, such as 'What forms of sodomy do you engage in?' and 'How often do you do it?' Matt didn't want to answer these. Frank didn't like it one bit either, and neither did I, but I thought we had to answer them to protect the case. If we had refused, it gave them an argument. They'd bring up the bullshit about blackmail and all the rest. So I told Matt, 'If you really want to take this case all the way, you're going to have to suffer a little indignity and invasion of your privacy. You don't have to sit there and let them harass you, but let's ask them in writing what they want you to tell them. Then they can pose their questions in writing, and we can reply the same way."

The result was the following extraordinary document, addressed to Special Agent Ramberger of the OSI Detachment at Langley, dated April 25, 1975, which the Air Force later presented in court:

"After consulting with my civilian attorney, David F. Addlestone, I have concluded that my constitutional right to privacy and the legitimate interests of the Air Force can be balanced by my submission of the following information about my sexual preference.

"My first homosexual experience was in approximately 1973. Since that time my sexual relations have been exclusively with other males. I have concluded that my sexual preference is entirely for other males and that I have no desire for heterosexual relationships.

"I have engaged in homosexual acts in Florida, Louisiana, Virginia and Washington, D.C. These acts have included mutual masturbation, anal intercourse and fellatio. My partners have all been persons about my age or slightly younger, but never younger than twenty-one years old to the best of my knowledge. My partners have included doctors, dentists, lawyers, and have without exception been respectable average citizens. I met them in the same fashion that a heterosexual of my same age would meet persons of the opposite sex. The acts have always occurred in a private home (off-base and off-duty) or in a hotel room if I happened to be staying in one at the time. Never have other persons been present.

"I have had sexual relations with two other members of the Air Force, one of whom has been discharged. Both of these persons did not work for me. As any responsible NCO, I would always refrain from such a relationship.

"At some point I wish to establish a permanent monogamous relationship with the 'right person.'"

Matlovich concluded the letter by declining to supply the specific names of his partners, by refusing the request for a search of his home, and by denying that he had ever been or was ever likely to be blackmailed.

With this letter in hand and the series of investigations by the OSI completed, the Air Force was finally ready to act. On May 20, 1975, Lt. Col. Charles R. Ritchie, commander, Langley Air Force Base, sent Matlovich a letter beginning, "Under the provisions of AFM 39-12, Chapter 2, Section H, Paragraph 2-104b(1), I am initiating action against you with a view to effecting your discharge from the United States Air Force." Ritchie then gave five reasons for this action.

The first was that on March 6 Matlovich wrote a letter to the Secretary of the Air Force stating his homosexuality. The second was that Matlovich told Technical Sergeant Michael Marotta, a co-worker from May 1973 to August 1974, that he was gay. According to Ritchie, Matlovich also told Marotta that he had read an article "by a doctor who claimed to be a homosexual and who was associated with the American Civil Liberties Union. You further advised Marotta that you had contacted the doctor and were told by him that you were ideal for a 'test case.'"

The third reason was that Sergeant Armando Lemos "suspected that you were a homosexual when he began to know you in November or December, 1972 at Hurlburt Field, Florida." Furthermore, Lemos related that Matlovich " 'frequently visited gay bars in Pensacola, Florida' and that [he] 'frequently talked about equality for homosexuals.' " Matlovich also placed "considerable emphasis" upon homosexual rights in his race relations course and entertained homosexual friends who visited his trailer, according to Lemos.

The fourth reason was that Matlovich told Special Agents Mault and Ramberger of the OSI that he was gay. The fifth was his letter to Ramberger.

After notifying Matlovich of his recommendation to furnish him with a general, or less than honorable, discharge, Ritchie then informed Matlovich of his rights: to use the appointed military counsel, to choose one of his own, to employ civilian counsel (which he would have to pay for out of his own pocket, "as funds are not available for payment of counsel fees"), to present his case before an administrative discharge board, to submit statements in his own behalf, and to waive the above rights.

Ritchie concluded, "You are entitled to and must undergo a complete medical examination in accordance with AFMs 53-5 and 160-1. Arrangements have been made for this examination and you will report to USAF Hospital, Langley at 0800 hours on 27 May 1975."

At this point, Addlestone, Jaenicke, and Matlovich decided to change their strategy. According to Matlovich:

"Previously, the strategy was that we would do no publicity whatsoever if the Air Force changed its mind and decided to keep me in. We wanted to convince the Air Force that publicity wasn't our goal; changing the policy was. But then Colonel Ritchie sent me the letter saying they were going to discharge me anyway, so we went ahead and did an interview with a woman from the *New York Times.* David Addlestone thought that with nothing left to lose it would benefit us to go public, but in a 'dignified' way."

The woman who wrote the story for the *Times,* Lesley Oelsner, told Leonard after completing the interview that she did not know when or even if the story would break — but it would probably be somewhere around Memorial Day. On Memorial Day,

May 26, therefore, Leonard went to a local bookstore to look for the story in the back pages of the *Times*. He saw nothing in the headlines, but when he picked up the paper and the bottom half fell down, he was astonished to find his story — and picture — on the front page.

In the article, Oelsner not only presented Matlovich's case to the public, she also informed them of his background, focusing on his lengthy path to self-acceptance. She included interviews with Frank Kameny and with Major General Jeanne Holm, a spokesperson for the Air Force, who provided opposing views of the military's ban on homosexuals. Oelsner also highlighted the case's potential significance:

"At stake are major, possibly competing, issues and rights — the military's interest in having rules it deems necessary to maintaining an adequate armed services system; the homosexual's constitutional rights to privacy and equal protection of the laws.

"Perhaps also at stake is the future of thousands of other service personnel. Leaders of the homosexual rights movement contend that there are, albeit under cover, as many homosexuals in the military as in civilian life; in the Hampton Roads area, at least, where Sergeant Matlovich is based, there seem to be hundreds."

The moment the *Times* article appeared, the case became a media event. As soon as Matlovich returned home, the phone was ringing off the hook. All the news networks wanted to interview him. CBS chartered a plane, interviewed him, and had him on the evening news. The *Washington Post* scrambled all over themselves, according to Addlestone, to get a big story in the next day. In the midst of this avalanche, Leonard's main concern was for his parents.

"I called home that same day and said to my mother, 'We've got to tell Dad right now, because CBS is going to be here in a half an hour for the evening news.' She said, 'It's not necessary. He already knows.' I asked, 'You told him?' And she replied, 'No, he read it in the morning newspaper.' So that's how my father found out.

"At first, I thought I'd probably never see him again. Like his father, he was always very authoritative. I can remember when I worshipped the very ground he walked on but also when I really hated him. When I was a kid, for example, I had to be in the house before dark, and if I ever didn't do what he said, that was it. So I've always felt freer to discuss things with my mother because I have a closer relationship with her. Anyway, in this particular case, I felt like I was challenging parental authority again.

"Besides, politcally, my father makes Genghis Khan look like Jesse Jackson. He's extremely conservative. Although my mother is from a conservative part of the country, Georgia, and my father is from what is considered a more tolerant part of the country, Pennsylvania, in reality you'd think it was the other way around. I just didn't think he could accept it.

"He didn't, either — at least not for a few hours. When he read the story in the paper he locked himself in the bedroom and cried. When he came out, however, that was it. He knew there was nothing he could do about it, and he decided to support me. He's been one of my biggest supporters ever since — a real champion. He's never heard me speak in person, and we've never really talked about my being gay, but I know that he has defended me on a number of occasions. And when I saw him again, after he found out, we actually hugged each other. It was the first time we had done that since I was a child."

According to Michael Bedwell, who was further removed from the situation and thus able to view it from a more critical perspective, the elder Matlovich's transformation was perhaps not quite so instantaneous or as thorough as Leonard would like to have believed:

"Leonard had an interesting relationship with his father. His father called him Sonny; Leonard called him Daddy. Their bond was much less emotional than that of Leonard and his mother — his dad was somewhat distant — but his father loved him just as much as his mother did. That was why Leonard's parents supported him. They wanted to believe he was doing something good.

"But support doesn't always mean acceptance. If Leonard's mother could have prevented him from becoming a gay activist, she would have. The only way I can understand her reaction is to compare it to my own mother's attitude when I was going to appear on television once: 'I love you, but I can't deal with what other people will say.' I think it was the same for her. Leonard's parents, like mine, came from a cultural milieu where they could never understand his being gay; they just accepted it as a handicap.

"When Leonard first came out, for instance, his mother said that she didn't really think he was gay. It was just some bandwagon he was on. They didn't understand that Leonard's activism stemmed directly from his faith in the things he was taught about liberty and freedom of choice in America. He took these things entirely literally. Fighting injustice, therefore, was just as natural to Leonard as sexual desire for a good-looking man. Fortunately, although Leonard's parents didn't understand why he did the things he did, they saw that other respectable people did. That meant a lot to them.

"That Leonard escaped this background is clearly a miracle. Many gay people haven't been so fortunate. They may have accepted themselves and come out of the closet, but they have remained just as racist and anti-Semitic as their parents. Leonard leapt beyond that. True, he did bring some things with him from his background, like his irrational anti-Communism and his vehement opposition to gun control. He was a complex person. But he had a sensitivity that enabled him to identify with other oppressed minorities. That, combined with his great sense of righteousness, later made him an effective spokesperson for the gay movement."

Reactions of others to the publicity differed from those of his parents. Most of his straight acquaintances, including many of his co-workers, were supportive. One who saw him in the dining hall almost turned a table over running up to shake Leonard's hand and to say how proud he was of Leonard, and that if there was anything he could do to let him know. A few were openly homophobic and didn't want to deal with him. Some were annoyed with him for giving the Air Force bad press.

Of the gay people on the base, many came around to his side at last — but for various reasons. Some who were afraid of him before suddenly couldn't get enough of him because of the media attention. But that didn't mean they cared about him, Leonard suspected — only that they cared about the publicity. These people he referred to as "star-fuckers," and he began telling friends that "there are far more star-fuckers than star-lovers in the world."

Of the many letters he received from strangers, most were encouraging. Only two of the thirty letters that arrived the first week were hostile. One gay World War II veteran wrote about suffering "the tortures of the damned" when he was in the military and thanked him profusely for his courage. However, he did receive threatening and obscene phone calls.

"I became accustomed very fast to those. It was usually obvious that they were from weirdos. But one phone call terrified me. The man who placed it was really good. He said, 'I'm not trying to scare you, but a group of men met last night, and they're coming to get you. They're going to cut your tongue and your balls off and put lye in your eyes. They have surgical instruments to do it with and something to stop the bleeding, because they don't want you to die. I can't tell you who I am, because I've got a wife and two kids, and if they find out I've talked to you, they'll come and get us. But please take care of yourself. I worry about you.' I was so terrified by that call that I began carrying a gun whenever I was off the base. But after about two weeks, I realized I was becoming what I was trying to fight, so I put the gun away.

"I was almost sorry I did. One night when I was living downtown in Hampton, I was in bed already when I heard a car pull up and three or four gunshots go off. Somebody shot at the house and drove off. I went outside, and so did all the neighbors, but we didn't see anything. I didn't call the police, though, and neither did anyone else because I was really afraid that had the military found out about it, they would have tried to move me back into the barracks, and I did not want to live there. I did not want to get into a situation where they could try to set me up again.

"That was still a problem, you see. Once the story broke, there was so much press around me that the military became very cautious. Had they done something stupid, the press would have swooped down on them. But they were still looking for things to use against me. My first sergeant, for instance, bluntly told me, 'If I were in charge of this, I'd get rid of you in a week. We'd set you up so fast, your head would swim. This whole thing is ridiculous.' That's why I had to be cautious too."

As far as David Addlestone was concerned, Matlovich could not be cautious enough.

"With the case becoming a media event, it took on a life of its own — which was dangerous for Matt. He had to be really careful what he said publicly, for the Air Force was going to use anything they could to shoot down his good-soldier reputation. This was really difficult for Matt, because he was basically a quiet, decent, average, good old American guy who was used to playing things honestly, and he didn't know how to react to being manipulated. Furthermore, he didn't know how to handle himself publicly.

"Once, for instance, there was a picture of him in the newspaper dancing in a gay bar, and that scared me. I thought that somehow it might hurt the case. Another time, he got a little testy with his boss, and they sort of got into it. It was the only spot on his record that they could possibly use against him, and I was afraid that they would. They could have brought in his boss to testify, 'Since he submitted his letter, he's been going around espousing civil rights for gays as well as his own case. Therefore he's become a less-effective member of the service.' That really concerned me, for we had kept our record really clean so far. It gave us a great deal of mileage on the exception policy. Fortunately, that testimony never came about."

On June 12, 1975, Colonel Schofield issued Matlovich's annual Airman Performance Report (APR) covering the period from June 14, 1974 to May 19, 1975. In it, both Captain Collins, the reporting official, and Schofield, the indorsing official, gave Matlovich the highest possible rating on a ten-point scale in the areas of "Performance of Duty," "Working Relations," "Training," "Supervision," and "Bearing." Only in two areas did the gay sergeant fall below perfection. In the areas of "Behavior" and "Acceptance of NCA Responsibility," Collins gave him a rating of six on the zero-to-nine scale. In the same areas, Schofield gave him a zero. The two superior officers concluded their report with an "Overall Evaluation." Collins gave Matlovich a seven; Schofield, amazingly, again gave him a zero.

They did this in spite of the ratings they gave him in the first five categories and in spite of an attached letter of evaluation from Major Arthur C. Patton, Chief of Race Relations at Langley, dated March 31, 1975. In that letter, Patton stated:

"[Matlovich's] initiative, dedication, and vigor all contributed to the successful training, in an outstanding manner, of 150 of the base population. Sgt. Matlovich showed superior leadership and innovative qualities. He introduced various new exercises to our program which we have adopted permanently into our curriculum. We received many favorable comments about his outstanding instructional ability in the delicate and sensitive area of Race Relations. STRENGTHS: Sgt. Matlovich consistently displayed a high level of loyalty, dedication, and initiative, which far exceeded the demands of the critical job assignment he performed in. OTHER COMMENTS: Sgt. Matlovich is an excellent team worker and performs superbly, free of even minimal supervision· He has unlimited potential as a career NCO He does all that is humanly possible to further the goals of the Department of Defense to reduce racial tensions and misunderstanding within the Armed Forces. He strongly supports Equal Opportunity and Treatment for Air Force personnel. I strongly recommend Sgt. Matlovich be promoted at the earliest possible opportunity."

Whether or not Patton knew of Matlovich's letter to the Secretary of the Air Force when he made this report on March 31 is unclear. Collins, however, was well aware of Leonard's standing when he concluded his own evaluation with the following comments:

"Sgt. Matlovich performed all assigned duties in an outstanding manner. He quickly mastered his new job responsibilities which proved to be extremely important. . . . His response to the pressure of this situation was commendable. . . . His performance was lauded by those who attended his classes. . . . STRENGTHS: Sgt. Matlovich has a great deal of enthusiasm for and dedication to his work. OTHER COMMENTS: Sgt. Matlovich is actively involved in and supportive of the Air Force Equal

Opportunity Program. However, his behavior is not in compliance with Air Force standards in that he has engaged in homosexual acts and has habitually associated with male persons known to him to be homosexuals. These actions detract from the overall image expected of an NCO."

It was left to Schofield to conclude, "Your personal conduct is below minimum acceptable standards. . . . If you believe this APR is inaccurate, unjust, or unfairly prejudicial to your career, you may apply for a review of the report under the provisions of AFR 31-11."

Matlovich's response was simple. He would see both Collins and Schofield at the administrative hearings — and then, most likely, in court.

5

The Battle Continues

A week before the administrative hearings were scheduled to begin in September, Matlovich's picture appeared on the cover of *Time* magazine. Although he was already a well-established figure on the gay political scene due to the extensive national coverage his case had received over the summer, the *Time* cover still created a sensation. Some were jealous of the attention garnered by the young upstart, a Johnny-come-lately to the gay movement in the eyes of many. One gay activist told him that *he* should have been on the cover rather than Leonard because he had paid his dues for so long. Matlovich simply replied that if he had that kind of power, he would gladly have arranged it.

Others were more generous, however. In fact, it was through Bruce Voeller, the founder and executive director of the National Gay Task Force at the time, that the editors of *Time* chose Matlovich for its cover in the first place. According to Voeller:

"My lover and I had been asked by *Time* if we were willing to be the cover story for their issue on homosexuals and the gay movement. We agreed, but then when we heard about Lenny, we told them that they ought to consider using him instead. I didn't know him, but I thought I could reach him. I thought the notion of having him as an openly gay person in uniform with his medals on would be just sensational. They thought it was a terrific idea and went with it. So I tracked him down and set things up. Sometime later, Lenny stayed with us at our home in New York, and we've been friends ever since."

Like Kameny and Addlestone before him, Voeller agreed that Leonard was the perfect role model to present before the American public.

"He was a godsend in that he did not fit the public perception of what gays are like. There he was, a very proud war hero with his ribbons, having been wounded and having worked his way up through the ranks. He was myth- and stereotype-defeating. It was quite wonderful to have that. From my point of view, he could serve as a dynamite role model for all kinds of people, both gay and non-gay. With Lenny's example, there was no way that people in the Armed Forces could maintain that homosexuals were automatically unfit for military service. That was of enormous importance to us.

"Like Lenny, I had grown up with no role model of any kind, and that kept me from accepting who I was until I was almost thirty. I didn't want my kids to grow up in the same situation. If they were gay, I wanted them to have the role models that we lacked. If they weren't gay, I wanted them to be exposed to gay people who were warm, good, and accomplished and who could serve as counterpoise to all the standard garbage that kids usually learn.

"Of course, a lot of people were pissed at Lenny because he was a military hero. The very virtue that I saw in him was considered by a lot of people in the movement to be anathema. These were the lower-case socialists and blue-denim elitists who dominated the movement in those days. They resented him because he showed a side to the world that most of them didn't."

Notes Michael Bedwell, Leonard's future roommate in both Washington, D.C. and San Francisco:

"Leonard was hurt deeply and repeatedly by some leaders of the movement. He was one of the bodies they walked over. He gave to the movement over and over again. He never said no. He paid his own way to events far more times than his way was paid for him. But his efforts were usually belittled by gay community leaders, who really missed the boat by refusing to look past Leonard's conservatism, his naivete, and his emotionalism. Instead of concentrating on these things, they should have concentrated and capitalized on those unique characteristics of his which attracted Middle Americans — the people who hold our present and our future in their hands.

"In my opinion, Leonard was the best poster boy the movement ever had. He had a gift. I traveled with him everywhere, and I saw all types of people relate to him. He was recognized and admired not only by gay people but by straight people as well. He was frequently asked for his autograph. Something about him made mainstream people feel comfortable with him.

"When he was on *Donahue* the first time, for instance, the younger women wanted to marry him and the older women wanted to mother him. They certainly never reacted this way to other leaders of the movement. It was fascinating. It probably helped that he was not stereotypically gay. He didn't give a damn about opera, he didn't know anything about musicals, and he knew nothing about film history. Furthermore, he didn't have an appreciation for camp, and when he went to the gym, his main interest there was to swim, not to work out. Perhaps that's why so many of the movement's leaders distrusted him. Nevertheless, he fulfilled a communal need. Gay people were desperate for a positive role model, and there were very few who were as willing to provide it as Leonard."

It came as a great shock to Matlovich that any gay person who had suffered discrimination as he had, no matter what their political persuasion, could be angry with him for his background. Having no knowledge of the gay liberation movement — having never even seen a gay newspaper until the summer of 1975 — he was unprepared for the kind of criticism he faced. It was in the straight press, he later claimed, that he received most of his positive publicity. It was in the gay press that he was called a "napalmer" and a "baby-bomber." He soon discovered that many gay people felt it was a mistake to fight for the right to serve in the military. It was a rare privilege, they argued, to be excluded. But he replied that it is never a privilege to be denied a right for whatever reason. It is simply an infringement of liberty.

Suddenly, Matlovich found himself fighting the Vietnam War all over again. In trying to justify his involvement to others (he had no need to justify it to himself), he criticized the policy of the American government, but for reasons which many of his listeners could not accept. His comments further angered his antagonists:

"In my opinion, what happened in Vietnam was criminal on our part. If Vietnam was worth being there, we should have fought to win it. If it wasn't worth winning, then we should not have been there. I believe that when you go to war and ask someone in your country to die, you have a moral obligation to end that war as fast as possible. And that means being willing to use everything in your arsenal, if need be, to protect your people. While you're at war, you have no consideration for the enemy, for as soon as you worry about the fate of the enemy, you're neglecting the lives of the people under your charge. You go for the jugular vein. After the war, after you've annihilated your enemy, you can show great mercy. You try to forgive and forget. But while that war is going on, you must fight that war with a commitment to win it.

"If there is a just God in Heaven, Kennedy, Johnson, Nixon, and to some part Ford will be burning in hell. And especially Congress, because they were wanton murderers. They sent American boys to Vietnam to fight a war, and then they tied their hands behind their backs. Someone would be shooting at us, and we used to have to call to get permission to fire back. I think that's immoral.

"The Vietnamese thought we were crazy for fighting a war in that manner, and I don't blame them. I also understand why My Lai happened. When each day you watch your buddies on both sides of you being blown away all because of some stupid orders to capture the same hill over and over again, you become very callous toward human life. You know it's only a matter of time before your number comes up.

"At the same time, I don't blame the protestors at home for doing what they did, because that's what America is all about. I never took the criticism personally when I was in Vietnam, and I never got any kind of personal abuse when in or out of uniform. Had I had my own children, my kids would not have gone to Vietnam, even though I spent three years there, for I thought it was an immoral war. I would have advised them to go to Canada or to jail, whatever their convictions were."

While Leonard was busy defending himself against attacks from the left of the socio-political spectrum, he was also assaulted from the right. The former came from a group of people he was trying to adopt as his own — gay men and lesbians; the latter came from a group he had once considered family — the Mormon Church. As soon as the church learned of Matlovich's challenge to the Air Force, they summoned him to an inquistion. "Dear Brother," they wrote on July 13, 1975, "You are hereby requested to appear before the High Council Court of this Stake . . . for investigation of alleged wrongdoing on your part involving infraction of the standards and rules of the church." He was instructed to bring witnesses, if desired, and was informed that the hearing would be held on August 1, 1975.

Matlovich attended the hearing and stated his intention to continue to pursue his case against the military. As a result, he received the following letters in quick succession:

August 27, 1975: "You were disfellowshipped by [the High Council Court of the Norfolk Stake] and are denied the privilege of participating in the full program of the Church until the disfellowship is terminated. You are encouraged to attend sacrament and auxiliary meetings, and public conference sessions, but you are not entitled to speak, offer public prayer, partake of the sacrament, or otherwise participate in these meetings. You should continue to pay your tithes and offerings, live in harmony with gospel standards, and seek for a return to fellowship in the Church. . . . We again express our love and concern for you as an individual and as a child of Our Father. . . . Ponder carefully the counsel you received at the court, pray often, and search the scriptures diligently."

September 12, 1975: "In view of your expressed decision to make no effort to change or correct the conditions which led to the High Council Court held on 1 August, it is felt to be necessary to reconvene that court."

October 7, 1975: "This is to formally advise you that the High Council Court of this Stake, convened on 27 September, to which you were summoned but did not appear, took action to excommunicate you from the Church of Jesus Christ of Latter Day Saints. You have stated your intention to continue activism in a practice which is abhorrent to and in direct violation of the laws of our Heavenly Father. . . . Our Heavenly Father loves you, brother Leonard, as we love and appreciate you. We are deeply concerned for your welfare and your eternal salvation, but our duty is clear. We urge you to study the scriptures and pray, that you may come to know the *truth*, and to ignore the rising popular clamor for liberal practices in conflict with God's laws and eternal practices."

Matlovich was unmoved by the church's pleas and unaffected by their decision to excommunicate him.

"When I walked into a gay bar for the first time, I went one direction and religion went the other. I realized then that religion was selling me a line of shit. They were saying things that weren't true. The church was telling me that being gay was bad, when I knew otherwise. How could I trust them after that? What other misinformation were they spreading? You know, they say, 'Three strikes and you're out.' Well, the first strike was the Catholic Church. The second was the Mormon Church. I didn't need a third to quit the game. I decided I'd make my own rules.

"I now regret my involvement with the Mormon Church. I regret every year that I wasted following a false church. I no longer believe in God, but I think I'm more of a Christian today than I ever was then. By that I mean I practice the ideals of Christianity now, whereas before I simply called myself a Christian. I believe in 'Love Thy Neighbor As Thyself,' for instance, and I obviously didn't before, judging by the way I treated blacks. I also believe in loving thyself, which took me a long time to learn. Yet Christianity teaches self-denial and self-flagellation. The only reason I would go to church now would be to cruise some hot man who interested me. And I refuse to go through the mumbo jumbo just to cruise someone."

In spite of the opposition from many gay leaders and the Mormon Church, Matlovich did his best to adjust to his role as a new kind of spokesperson for the gay movement. The vast majority of gay people to whom he spoke responded to his call warmly. Leonard soon discovered that he had a natural talent for public speaking; he spoke from the heart, with sincerity and conviction. As a result, he continued to get more and more involved in the movement. He crisscrossed the country, speaking to a wide variety of groups — gay political organizations, university and high school associations, television and radio audiences, and church groups. He claimed he never turned down a speaking engagement. One of his greatest triumphs, he continued, was a speech he gave at Columbia University.

"The woman who spoke before me gave a talk that was mediocre at best, but she got a standing ovation. Then when I was introduced, there was cold silence. I heard a few boos in the audience. But when I left the stage, I left half of them standing and half of them booing, which I considered a great success. At least half the audience came around." Another success was his speech at the Gay Pride Parade in New York City in June. According to *Time*, he broke down and cried. Said Matlovich at that time, "I found myself, little nobody me, standing up in front of tens of thousands of gay people. And just two years ago I thought I was the only gay in the world. It was a mixture of joy and sadness. It was just great pride to be an American, to know I'm oppressed but able to stand up there and say so."

In the course of his travels that summer, many new experiences awaited the gay Air Force sergeant from South Carolina. At a Catholic school in Minnesota, someone threw rocks at him on stage. Leonard saw it as a challenge rather than as a threat, and he knew just how to respond. He used his own experiences as a Catholic school alumnus to make the students feel guilty. Later, he conjectured that the person who threw the rocks was probably trying to compensate for his own sexual insecurities.

In Chicago, a morning talk show host was less violent but

equally homophobic. The host couldn't get the microphone on his collar adjusted, so Leonard reached over to help him. Just then, the red light on the camera appeared, and Matlovich and the host were broadcast live all over Chicago in what appeared to be an awkward embrace. The host, fearful for his image, quickly picked up a copy of *Time* featuring Matlovich's picture, struck him with it, and said, "Get away from me." The host was not amused, but Matlovich couldn't stop laughing.

Another time, in England, Matlovich spoke to the Campaign for Homosexual Equality, a leftist gay group. He was continually heckled because he was a veteran. One man in particular kept interrupting his speech. Finally, Leonard stopped speaking and asked, "Is there a cowboy in the house?" No one answered, so he repeated his question. When someone replied, "All right, I'm a cowboy," Matlovich said, "Good. Then would you please ride this ass out of here?" The audience fell totally silent, and Leonard continued his speech, if not to acclaim, then at least with respect.

To help pay for these trips (as well as for expenses related to his court battle), Matlovich relied on a group called Friends of Matt, the only organization authorized to collect funds on his behalf other than Bruce Voeller's National Gay Task Force. Friends of Matt was established by two men from Washington, D.C., Richard Maulsby and Paul Kuntzler, who had been involved in community affairs, starting with the Gay Activist Alliance, since the early Seventies. They saw the Matlovich case not only as a way to help a worthy cause but also as a means to rejuvenate the gay movement, which they felt had grown stultified by then. As soon as they heard about the case, therefore, they began planning a large-scale fundraiser, which they envisioned as a one-time affair. They held the fundraiser in late October at Lost and Found, a popular Washington, D.C. disco, and cleared approximately five thousand dollars. Recalls Maulsby:

"By today's standards, that's not that much money, but more important than the money was the enthusiasm that was created by the event. It enhanced our sense of community by involving people in gay politics who had not been involved before, particularly bar owners and gay business leaders who had looked

askance at gay activists as flaming radical types carrying placards and shouting slogans. It became a much more acceptable,
mainline, middle-class thing to do. That's what I see as the real
significance of the event and of Leonard's case.

"The fundraiser had another equally-important and long-
lasting effect. It became the basis for forming the Gertrude Stein
Democratic Club in January 1976, and two years later it became
the nucleus for our struggle against Anita Bryant's 'Save Our
Children' campaign. In fact, much of the power we have today in
Washington stems from our association with Leonard's cause."

Unfortunately, the event sponsored by Voeller and the National Gay Task Force earlier that summer was not as successful.
Voeller contacted the leadership of the Islanders Club, a group of
affluent gay travelers, and enlisted their help in organizing a
fundraiser on Fire Island. The Islanders enthusiastically contributed cases of pink champagne left over from one of their trips
and set up buffet tables on a special part of the beach. However,
said Voeller:

"It was kind of disappointing and embittering for all of us.
We threw, by all accounts, the biggest such event that had ever
happened at the Island. Hundreds of people came. Everybody
wanted to shake hands, meet, and touch Lenny. We knew, of
course, that people wouldn't be carrying money in their bathing
suits, so we compiled a mailing list instead. Lenny and I then
drafted an appeal and did the mailings, but only a couple of hundred dollars came in. It put a very sour taste in my mouth and in
his about the lack of interest or concern by so many people on
the Island. If Lenny, who had just been on the cover of *Time* as
the great hero of the day, couldn't raise money in support of his
campaign, then no one could. It was just outrageous."

The Fire Island affair was not the only financial disappoint-
ment Matlovich was to face. Far more serious than the lack of interest some showed was the greed others displayed. As soon as
news of his fight with the Air Force spread across the country,
people unknown to Matlovich began holding fundraisers supposedly on his behalf but without his knowledge or consent. Matlovich was appalled. When people told him they had attended
fundraisers for him, he suggested they get their money back, for

he knew nothing about it. He was shocked to discover the extent of the problem.

That wasn't all. Speaking engagements were planned and tours were arranged without contracts or confirmation. When Leonard didn't show up in two places at once, people got furious with him. There was almost a lawsuit between sponsors in Seattle and San Francisco who expected him to speak at the same time, Leonard claimed. But once again, he pleaded ignorance. Swamped with phone calls, invitations, and requests for interviews, endorsements, speaking engagements, and benefits, Leonard was rapidly losing control of the situation. Notes Addlestone, "He was being turned into a media star. Everybody in the world wanted to use him. Everybody wanted a piece of him. And he didn't know how to handle it."

In an article entitled "Cannibalization of a Hero," which appeared in the *Advocate*, a national gay and lesbian newsmagazine, in late 1975, writer Sasha Gregory-Lewis called this state of affairs "the Matlovich mess." Wrote Gregory-Lewis, "It seemed as if every gay individual in the country felt he had a right to the gay celebrity's time. They acted as if they owned him. Citizen Matlovich became property Matlovich." When Matlovich didn't produce, continued the author, gay community leaders throughout the country abandoned his cause and "went sour" on him. As a result, the Air Force sergeant who never sought celebrity in the first place became "worn out, tired [and] confused" by the end of the year.

Gregory-Lewis placed much of the blame for "the Matlovich mess" on the shoulders of a disabled veteran named Al Seviere, a man Matlovich met whom "he felt he could trust, who would stand by him." In retrospect, Matlovich agreed with Gregory-Lewis's assessment:

"Al Seviere was a knight in shining armor to me when I met him. He was an absolutely gorgeous individual who appeared right when all this craziness was going on. In two months, however, he almost destroyed me. He created a great deal of bad press for me, because he turned into a manager and handled all my phone calls at a time when I wasn't paying close attention. I didn't realize until later how many problems he had. He was a paranoid schizophrenic, and I had never had any experience with a paranoid schizophrenic before. Unfortunately, my heart and my brain weren't functioning together. My heart had a crush on Al, and my mind knew that something wasn't right. It was just chaos.

"It ended when David Goodstein [then the publisher of the *Advocate* and a friend of Matlovich] said that if I didn't shape up my act, he was going to tear me apart in his newspaper. I realized then that things must be very wrong. So I told Al to get out of my life. He responded by threatening to throw my best friend out of a fourteen-story building. Then I sent a letter to the *Advocate* saying that this man did not represent me any longer and neither did anyone else, for I was no longer soliciting donations. I did, however, retain a professional agency to book speaking engagements for me, Harry Walker, Inc. of New York City. For a while, I also considered establishing an organization to be called the Matlovich Foundation for Civil Liberties. The purpose of this organization would be to hire a lobbyist for federal gay rights bills, to help others to fight their own court battles, and also to launch a media campaign, but nothing ever came of that.

"The reason all this affected me so much is that one of the only things I have in the world that I treasure is my good name, and I *have* managed to maintain that. When your name is associated with something that isn't true or real, you get upset about it. You just can't help it. I did learn one thing from all this, though. When you find yourself catapulted into the press, when you become a national media figure, you have to be very, very careful."

One of the insiders to "the Matlovich mess" was Michael Bedwell.

"The first time I ever heard of Leonard was when I saw him on *The Tom Snyder Show*. He was still in the Air Force then, and I was involved in a gay group at Indiana University, getting ready to put on a conference that Halloween weekend. I was really impressed with him, so I called him the next day in Virginia and asked him to speak at the conference. He agreed and suggested that we meet in Chicago, where he was appearing on *Donahue*, to discuss it.

"Leonard was just becoming involved with Al Seviere then, and already he was having problems with Al. He didn't talk about them in Chicago, but later, at the conference, Leonard drew me aside and said, 'Al is controlling my life too much, and I don't know how to distance myself from him. You don't have a permanent job. You organized the conference well. Would you be interested in working for me?'

"I was quite taken aback, not only by the offer but also by the surprising psychodrama that was taking place between Leonard and Al. Leonard warned me that Al would try to talk me out of taking the job, but he said that I should not let that discourage me. I told him I had to wrap some things up first, and he said, 'Fine. Meet me in New York in a couple of weeks.'

"The agreement was that I would help arrange speaking engagements for Leonard. By this time, he had been discharged, and the plan was to raise money on a barnstorming tour of the country. But Al was creating too many problems. Leonard's friends and advisors recognized that Al was a threat to the movement. Several times they attempted to discredit Al — with justification. But Leonard wouldn't listen. Once he got so furious with them at a dinner party for interfering in his private life that he insisted they all leave. He was in love with Al and couldn't see that Al was blackmailing him emotionally. Al was using Leonard as a meal ticket.

"For a while, Leonard didn't know who to trust. I was one of the ones who tried to tell Leonard that Al was decreasing his effectiveness, but Leonard only replied, 'Al warned me this would happen.' Eventually, however, even Leonard recognized that things were seriously wrong. The evidence against Al, including missing checks, tantrums, and psychiatrists' bills, was undeniable. Finally, one night Leonard blew up and screamed at Al, 'You're destroying my life. You're using and embarrassing me. I can't stand you. I never want to hear from you again!'

"Within twenty-four hours, however, Leonard was back on the phone with Al. He even rehired him and told me that I could go back to Indiana if I wanted. Instead, I went to New York to a conference there and discussed Al with Frank Kameny and others. They said there was nothing to be done. So after the conference, I went back to Indiana. I didn't see Leonard again for about a year.

"I never blamed Leonard for that. I felt sorry for him. He had been out such a short time and was incredibly naive. He was a babe in the wood who trusted everyone, and Al was the first person who responded to him emotionally — or so he thought. Still, it was a shame, for when one hero is discredited, it's hard for people to believe in the next one."

For Bruce Voeller, "the Matlovich mess" served to highlight the difficulties Leonard faced as a political neophyte suddenly thrust into the national spotlight:

"Lenny had some major problems early on in that he was catapulted into intense visibility and was called upon suddenly, as were several other people in that period (but he perhaps most strongly and clearly with the least preparation for it), to fill a role as a nationally known figure rather than as just another guy in the Armed Services. He was expected to be articulate and knowledgeable on TV and with the press and in conferences and meetings.

"Of course, it took him some time to learn his way around, to learn the history of the gay movement, and to master some of the basic argumentation and rhetoric that the movement had developed. In the process, he made some mistakes, understandably enough, which limited his ability to be the ultimate gay leader and which isolated him somewhat.

"A lot of times, for instance, he didn't see all the many layers and complexities that you have to weigh before you speak out or make a decision at some conference or meeting. The upshot is that he went off kind of half-cocked any number of times to a bad end, and that decreased the impact and the effect that he had in shaping the politics, the structure, the goals, and the directions of the gay movement.

"Nevertheless, he was basically a very decent, generous, and well-intentioned person who wasn't into games or trickery or a lot of the stuff that too many people have been into. He had enormous guts to do the things he did and to play the part he did. Overall, he made a major contribution to the growth and development of the movement."

In the midst of all this "craziness," at 0900 hours on September 16, 1975, at Langley, the Air Force convened its administrative hearing. Matlovich was represented by his defense attorneys, Jaenicke, Addlestone, and Hewman. The Air Force was represented by prosecutors Lt. Col. James E. Applegate and Capt. Edmund G. Flynn. A five-member Administrative Discharge Board served as the military equivalent of a jury, and Col. Robert E. Shank, the legal advisor, served as the equivalent of a judge.

On the first day of the trial, Addlestone conducted a *voir dire* — an examination of the board to determine its impartiality. Each was asked a series of questions: what had they read about homosexuality, did they view homosexuality as a sin or an illness, did they believe that homosexuals impair morale in the service, and did they think that homosexuals try to recruit straight people into their ranks? According to Martin Duberman in an article for the *New York Times Magazine* dated November 9, 1975, all of the board members "seemed candid, even earnest, in their responses." Nevertheless, they responded with so many "I don't know's" and "maybe's" that during a recess following the *voir dire*, wrote Duberman, "the civilian press corps tut-tutted over the officers' equivocation, ignorance and bigotry." In his opinion, "three of the five officers were genuinely unsure of their feelings about homosexuality and were open to hearing evidence. The other two [were] decidedly homophobic." Whatever the state of their true feelings, Addlestone challenged none of them "for cause."

Defense attorney Susan Hewman then filed a motion to dismiss. She argued that the regulation authorizing the hearings, AFM 39-12, was unconstitutional, in that it violated the right to privacy, due process, and equal protection under the law guaranteed by the First, Fifth, and Ninth Amendments to the Constitution. As a precedent, Hewman pointed to the landmark decision by the Civil Service Commission on July 3, 1975, that an employee may not be dismissed solely on the basis of homosexual conduct. Legal Advisor Shank promptly denied this motion and threw out the unconstitutionality argument.

Following this, the prosecution began calling witnesses to the stand. The first was Sergeant Armando Lemos, who met

Leonard in 1971 when Matlovich was in charge of the electric shop at Hurlburt Field, Florida. Although Lemos's statements about Matlovich's homosexuality were cited in the Air Force letter informing Matlovich of the decision to initiate action against him, at the hearings Lemos testified that Leonard's homosexuality had not affected their relationship and that he still considered the defendant an excellent instructor and serviceman.

Col. John N. Schofield, the head of the Drug and Alcohol Abuse and Race Relations programs at Langley, was the next witness for the prosecution. He stated his belief that Matlovich's ability to perform as a race relations instructor had been "totally impaired" by his admission of homosexuality. Furthermore, he said, Matlovich was no longer qualifed to serve in any capacity in the Air Force due to the bad image he presented.

Technical Sergeant Michael Marotta, whose statements were also cited in the letter of notification to Matlovich, was the third to be called to the stand. Under questioning by Jaenicke, Marotta voiced his opinion that Leonard's homosexuality would make him a better instructor than ever for having at last come to terms with himself. Sounding more like a witness for the defense than for the prosecution, Marotta praised Matlovich's dedication and skill.

At this point, one member of the Administrative Discharge Board, Col. David Glass, asked for a closed hearing to state his objections to the way the case was being handled. Both Glass and another member of the board, Major Phillip K. Heacock, then questioned the competence of the prosecution for bringing to the stand witnesses who supported Matlovich's case rather than hindered it. Prosecutor Applegate's response was swift. He challenged the two for cause, and they were summarily dismissed.

Before resting his case, Applegate also called Special Agent Ramberger of the OSI to the stand and introduced into evidence both letters that Matlovich had sent to the Air Force — the initial one stating his homosexuality and the other providing the details.

For the defense, Addlestone called to the stand two experts in the field of sexual behavior. The first, Dr. John W. Money, was the co-founder of the Gender Identity Clinic at Johns Hopkins University, the head of the psycho-hormonal research unit there, president of the Society for the Scientific Study of Sex, and the author of a dozen books and hundreds of articles. He testified that he had interviewed Matlovich and had found him to be "extraordinarily stable," with a history of having stood up well under pressure. He also discussed theories of sexual identity as well as the blackmail issue.

The other sex expert was Dr. Wardell B. Pomeroy, a psychologist associated with the Kinsey Institute for thirteen years and the author of several books. According to Duberman in the *New York Times Magazine*, Pomeroy gave evidence that sounded like a Homosexual Studies introductory course, which was "so obvious as to be banal [to] most reasonable, or reasonably well-informed, people." No, Pomeroy said, the majority of homosexuals do not wish to convert heterosexuals; no, they are not likely to molest children; yes, they stand up as well as anyone to pressure; and no, homosexuality is neither unnatural or immoral — once the terms have been defined adequately.

Addlestone even called to the stand Dr. Douglass H. Chessen, the Air Force psychiatrist who had interviewed Matlovich four times and concluded that he was "fully capable of performing his military duties." Also appearing for the defense was Sgt. Cornell Langford, a black race relations counselor at Langley who called Matlovich "the best," and Matlovich himself, who stated that he wanted to stay in the Air Force but refused to agree not to engage in any more homosexual acts, "for that's asking me to be celibate for the rest of my life." He would, however, sign a contract never to make another public statement, for publicity was never the point in the first place.

Before resting his case, Addlestone introduced into evidence over fifteen hundred student critiques of their former instructor. Of these, ninety-three percent rated Matlovich better than any of their previous instructors. Addlestone also reiterated his argument, which he had made throughout the trial, that based on his "twelve years of unblemished, distinguished service for his country in peace and war," Matlovich qualified for the exception to the Air Force policy on homosexuality contained in AFM 39-12. Before adjourning, reported Duberman of the *Times*, Col.

Shank, the legal advisor, "in his formal charge at the close of the hearing, sternly warned the officers that their sole duty was to apply current Air Force regulations, not to pass judgment on their merits, and certainly not to consider the broader constitutional issues that might be involved. By that narrow construction, Matlovich had little chance."

The remaining three members on the Administrative Discharge Board wasted little time reaching a decision. On September 16, 1975, after four days of testimony and argument, they unanimously recommended that Matlovich be given a general, or less than honorable, discharge. Two weeks later, on September 30, the commander of Langley completed his review of the procedings and determined that Leonard's discharge should be upgraded to honorable. On October 20, the Secretary of the Air Force, John McLucas, issued a "final and conclusive" decision agreeing with the Langley commander. Finally, on October 21, Matlovich was officially notified of his discharge. He was barred from re-enlistment and was informed that he was unentitled to severance pay or to retirement benefits.

The very next day, October 22, Addlestone appealed to Judge Gerhard Gesell of the United States District Court, Washington, D.C. for a temporary restraining order barring the discharge. "Because the government had made the mistake of saying the Secretary of the Air Force would actually deal with the case," explained Addlestone, "that gave us venue in the District of Columbia as opposed to the Fourth Circuit, which was a significantly different place to litigate. Not only was it more convenient for us, but it also had better case law and more sympathetic judges." Unfortunately for Addlestone's client, Judge Gesell was sympathetic — but not enough. In denying Addlestone's request, he stated:

"It appears to the Court that the Plaintiff has not demonstrated the type of irreparable injury which would justify the extraordinary intervention of the Court into the course of his discharge proceedings.

"The Court is also well aware of what appears to be a clear but unfortunate trend in the decisions of the Supreme Court and the Court of Appeals for the District of Columbia strictly limiting the opportunity for servicemen in the modern Army to raise constitutional issues such as privacy, the Fourth Amendment, the First Amendment, and other matters of that kind.

"So I feel — trying as best I can to sense the trend of the decisions in the higher courts — that the chances of ultimate success in this particular matter are not great. . . .

"I would simply comment that in this test case, which I assume and believe has been handled in good faith by both sides, involving a man of exceptional qualifications for the military, who has served his country well both in combat and in peacetime, that the Air Force is proceeding by the book when possibly a more compassionate view could have been taken of this situation pending the resolution of these serious and important issues. But that feeling that I have, and I have it quite strongly, does not warrant my departing from the standard legal requirements for temporary restraining order; and I will not enter one."

All was not lost, however, for Gesell did set a hearing at the District Court level, which was delayed for several months by a *pro forma* appeal to the Air Force's Board for Correction of Military Records, a bureaucratic procedure which was necessary but unsuccessful.

Because he anticipated the defeat, Leonard was not discouraged by the outcome of the administrative hearing. If anything, he was relieved.

"I'll never forget the day I drove out the gates for the last time. I was so relieved. I had made it to the end of the hearings, and the Air Force hadn't managed to entrap me or to discredit my record, no matter how hard they tried. It was a fabulous feeling. From March through October, the case remained exactly what we wanted it to be, an uncompromised test of the military's policy excluding gay servicemen and women. Naturally, I was sorry to have lost, but I hadn't given up hope. I still believed we could take this case to the civil courts and win." Addlestone agreed. As he recalls, following the appeal to the Board of Correction for military records:

"Gesell put the case on the fast track. He said, 'I want certain information from the Air Force. You had better be prepared to respond to this, that, and the other.' He was giving projections that he thought the Air Force hardly had any justification for their policy. Granted, I was reading between the lines, but just because he didn't grant us the temporary restraining order didn't mean he wasn't going to rule in our favor when we took the case to the District Court."

Addlestone and Matlovich's optimism and determination were soon to be tested, however. A few months later, in May 1976, the United States Supreme Court refused to hear what was intended to be a landmark test case, *Doe v. Commonwealth's Attorney for the City of Richmond*. By refusing, the Court let stand a lower court decision upholding Virginia's antiquated sodomy laws. Homosexuals, they silently concurred, had no right to engage in consensual sexual behavior, not even in the privacy of their own homes.

It was a major setback for the gay rights movement, and it could not have come at a worse time for Matlovich, for it directly influenced Gesell's decision in his own case. On June 11, 1976, Gesell disagreed with Leonard's claim that his discharge was unconstitutional. "[The] record clearly demonstrates," Gesell wrote, "that the questioned regulation is Constitutional, and that defendants' actions in discharging plaintiff [i.e. Matlovich] were lawful and proper, and not arbitrary and capricious." On this same date, Gesell ordered the Air Force to clarify their position on the exception provision of the regulations.

Then, on July 16, 1976, after carefully examining the evidence and testimony presented at Matlovich's Air Force hearing, Gesell reached his final decision. He reluctantly sided in favor of the Air Force — but not without praising Leonard first.

"[Sgt. Matlovich] has had a most commendable, highly useful service in the military over a long period of time, starting with the Air Force in 1963. . . . Here is a man who volunteered for assignment to Vietnam, who served in Vietnam with distinction, who was awarded the Bronze Star while only an Airman First Class, engaged in hazardous duty on a volunteer basis on more than one occasion, wounded in a mine explosion, revolunteered, has excelled in the Service as a training officer, as a counseling officer and in the various social action programs and race-relation programs of the military, and has at all times been rated at the highest possible ratings by his superiors in all aspects of his performance, receiving in addition to the Bronze Star, the Purple Heart, two Air Force Commendation Medals and a Meritorious Service Medal.

"[However,] legitimate state interest [is] apparent here. . . . It cannot be said that the Air Force regulation at issue here is so irrational that it may be branded arbitrary and, therefore, a deprivation of Plaintiff's liberty, interest in freedom to choose his own sexual preferences, or the like. . . .

"This is a distressing case. It is a bad case. It may be that bad cases will make bad law. Having spent many months dealing with aspects of this litigation, it is impossible to escape the feeling that the time has arrived or may be imminent when branches of the Armed Forces need to reappraise the problem which homosexuality unquestionably presents in the military context.

"The Services are admittedly involved in matters of immediate and clear importance. They not only have problems with respect to performing the obvious military task but there are moral, religious and privacy overtones that cannot and should not be overlooked.

"We all recognize that by a gradual process there has come to be a much greater understanding of many aspects of homosexuality. Public attitudes are clearly changing. Some state legislatures have already acted to reflect these changing public attitudes, moving more in the direction of tolerance. Physicians, church leaders, educators and psychologists are able now to demonstrate that there is no standard, no preconceived stereotype of a homosexual, which, unfortunately, some of the Air Force knee-jerk reaction to these cases would suggest still prevails in the Department. . . .

"In the light of increasing public awareness and the more open acceptance of what is in many respects essentially a matter of private sexual conduct, it would appear that the Armed Forces might well be advised to move toward a more discriminatory and informed approach to these problems, as has the Civil Service Commission in its treatment of homosexuality within the civilian sector of Government employment. . . .

"The Armed Forces have been in many ways leaders in social

experimentation and in their adaptability to changing community standards. No one, for example, who has studied the civil rights movement and the striving of blacks for opportunity will ever fail to recognize that the Armed Forces, more than any branch of Government and far ahead of the private sector in this country, led to erasing the stigma of race discrimination. It is one of the great high points of military accomplishment.

"Here another opportunity is presented. While the Court has reached its conclusions, as a judge must do, on the law, I hope it will be recognized that . . . the Court, individually, for what it is worth, has reached the conclusion that it is desirable for the military to re-examine the homosexual problem, to approach it in perhaps a more sensitive and precise way."

6

Settling In

Win or lose, Leonard's courage was already having a profound effect on other gay people in the military. On May 23, 1975, three days before his story hit the front page of the *New York Times*, Staff Sergeant Rudolf S. Keith, Jr., an aircraft maintenance specialist at Dover Air Force Base with six and a half years of service, discussed his homosexual orientation in front of twenty-nine people during a race relations seminar. Soon thereafter, following Matlovich's example, Keith went public with a series of radio interviews. At the same time, two U.S. Army WACs from Fort Devens, Massachusetts, PFC Barbara Randolph and Pvt. Debbie Watson, declared their homosexuality. All three joined Matlovich on stage at the June 29 Gay Pride Rally in New York City.

The military was as intolerant of their demands to continue to serve in the Armed Forces as it was of Matlovich's. On September 23, 1975, following an administrative hearing, Keith was discharged from the Air Force. Privates Randolph and Watson were also discharged from the Army, despite the intervention of the ACLU. These three thus joined the growing list of gay military exiles. According to the *Advocate* in a story dated July 2, 1975, "Over 50,000 veterans have been issued other than Honorable Discharges since the beginning of the Vietnam War, many of them, no doubt, simply for being gay." In one way, however, Keith, Randolph, and Watson could count themselves lucky. Prior to mid-1974, all discharges carried a Separation Program Number (SPN). SPN 46D was the designation for "Unsuitability — Sexual Deviate." Although these were supposedly secret, they were often leaked to potential employers, creditors, and the like. Many gay servicemen and -women found their careers hampered as a result.

While others fought and lost their separate battles, Matlovich tried to carry on with his own. Unfortunately, the former Air Force sergeant soon faced a disappointing and unexpected development. Contrary to its original intentions, the ACLU decided not to sponsor his appeal. Explains Addlestone:

"At first, our intentions were to go all the way. But then, right in the middle of the case when we were in federal court, the Supreme Court affirmed that Virginia sodomy case. In addition, all these horrendous decisions involving other military cases came down, and Judge Gesell ruled against us. Now, the way I read his decision was that he was telling us, 'Look, you are going to make things worse if you appeal this case. I've got all the sympathy in the world for you, but you are going to make bad law.' I couldn't help but agree.

"I certainly didn't want that to happen. If we lost, the headlines were going to scream out in the provinces that the courts say it's unconstitutional to be queer. Even if we did win, we would probably win on narrow grounds, and the risk wasn't worth it. I thought it was time to take the issue out of the judicial arena, at least for the time being.

"At the time, remember, the political processes seemed to be working in favor of gay rights. Sodomy statutes were being repealed in many states, and the gay community was doing a very good job politically. They were doing their homework and making great strides. Since courts involved in civil liberties cases cannot ignore the political process, they were eventually going to have to deal with the issue in a more positive light. So in the meantime, why upset the political process with the loss of this case?

"I circulated this idea among eight or nine lawyers who I

respected, and basically everybody agreed with me, including the local legal director of the ACLU. Since I had about eight months of professional life invested in the case, this was a really hard decision — but I felt we shouldn't go foward. Frank Kameny was pissed off as hell, of course. And Leonard argued with me. 'Look, David,' he said, 'we can't turn tail and run. I have to go on with this thing.' I said, 'I respect that. I understand where you're coming from. I'm just rendering you my legal advice. But since this is now a political case, the gay community has to decide how you are going to proceed, not me.'"

Determined to pursue the case through the courts despite Addlestone's advice, Matlovich looked elsewhere for representation. Through a mutual acquaintance, he met Carrington Boggan, an attorney with a private practice in New York City. Boggan was a former member of the Gay Activist Alliance as well as the general counsel for a gay rights organization called Lambda Legal Defense and Education Fund. For years, Boggan had been involved in various gay rights cases, including a number of administrative military proceedings concerning upgrades of less-than-honorable discharges.

At the time, Boggan was also handling a similar case which had been taken on by Lambda — one involving a gay Naval officer named Vernon Berg. Boggan had handled that case from the beginning, starting with the military hearing and continuing in the civil courts. When the Matlovich matter came to his attention, he presented it to Lambda to see if they would be interested in sponsoring the appeal. In view of their limited resources, they felt that one military case was all they could handle at the time. Therefore, Boggan took the case on an individual *pro bono* basis, asking Leonard to pay only for the reproduction of briefs and other out-of-pocket expenses. "I took the case," explains Boggan, "because it was important. It was not one that should have been allowed to lapse because no one was willing to handle the appeal."

Boggan accepted the case in 1976 and took it to the U.S. Court of Appeals. If Leonard expected a quick decision, he was to be disappointed once again. Not until December 1978, over two years later, was a decision reached. In the meantime, he had to get on with his life — as a civilian.

In late 1975, following his discharge from the Air Force, Matlovich moved from Hampton, Virginia, to Washington, D.C., where he found a place to live with a gay couple who were members of the Metropolitan Community Church, a national gay protestant church founded in the late 1960s. Embarking on a career as a professional gay activist, he lived on approximately $4,500 a year for the next three years, earning his money entirely through speaking engagements arranged by his agent, Harry Walker, Inc. of New York. It was not a deliberate career choice but the natural outgrowth of the many demands placed upon his time. Despite the "Matlovich mess," he was still swamped with requests to appear before various organizations across the country. Accustomed to service but unable to serve the Air Force any longer, he chose a new direction and devoted his energies to the gay rights movement instead.

By taking charge of his own affairs or assigning them to professionals rather than to sycophants and boyfriends, Leonard was able to regain the trust of the gay community and to end the "craziness" of the Matlovich mess. In time, he learned to deal with the attention he received and to judge the difference between those who were truly interested in him and those who were interested only in his status as a media star. While he remained a controversial figure due to his unrelenting conservative political beliefs in all areas other than gay rights (in Washington he registered as a Democrat "out of necessity" but remained a Goldwater Republican at heart), he was regarded by many as a hero, the community's first national gay hero. It was a role he regarded ambivalently.

"When I could see that I helped people and was effective, I enjoyed it. When people came up to me and said, 'You're one of the reasons I had the courage to come out of the closet,' I thought it was great. Also, the quality of my bed partners definitely increased when I started speaking around the country, and I didn't mind that either. But I took it for what it was worth, and I tried not to let it affect me. I really didn't have a big ego. I never asked to be a leader in the first place. What I wanted, more than anything else in the world, was to have a lover, a house in the suburbs with a front yard and a picket fence, a dog and a cat, joint income tax returns, and a Safeway around the corner. That would have made me happy. That was my goal in life. If I had had that, you probably never would have heard my name in the papers again."

Journalist Randy Shilts was quick to realize this when he first met Matlovich in December 1975, soon after Leonard's picture appeared on the cover of *Time*. Shilts had only recently graduated from the University of Oregon journalism school and was then serving as the Pacific Northwest correspondent for the *Advocate*. He met Leonard at a meeting of the Dorian Club, a group of gay businessmen, in Seattle. Matlovich was the guest speaker, and both he and Shilts were staying at the home of local businessman and activist Charles Brydon. Recalls Shilts:

"Over the course of that weekend, Brydon's living room was filled with guys who wanted to talk to Lenny. And of course they all wanted to go to bed with him. I'll never forget those people. There were so many who were in the closet and who still couldn't figure out how to deal with it. They turned to Lenny as some kind of guru. People looked to him as if he could fix something. It was a strange role he was thrust into.

"Ironically, while people wanted something from him, he wanted something in return and couldn't seem to find it. You see, there's always been this side of Lenny that's always been very lonely. I remember when he was done with his speech, before they asked questions, he said, 'I know what the first question is going to be, and the answer is, 'No, but I'm looking.' Everybody laughed, and Lenny said, 'I say that because everybody always asks if I have a boyfriend.' It was interesting, because nobody *had* asked yet, and it was a fairly brazen way of saying, 'I'm available.'"

As Leonard's best friend, Michael Bedwell was well aware from the beginning that love was one of most important things in Leonard's life. Leonard's search for a partner was so intense, notes Bedwell, that it was almost obsessive. According to Bedwell, this obsession might have grown out of the lack of warmth in the relationship of Leonard and his father, at least when Leonard was young, but he admits that this is only a theory. He prefers to explain only what he learned for himself:

"Like many gay people, Leonard was addicted to the idea of the perfect lover. Unfortunately, he didn't know how to go about achieving a long-lasting, stable relationship. One of the difficulties was his lack of experience. Because Leonard came out late, he had this subconscious desire to make up for lost time. When he finally stepped out of the closet, he left the guilt and shame of his past completely behind. He was one hundred percent queer, and he wanted to do something about it.

"So he had a lot of sex. It wasn't as much sex as he would have liked, but it was as much sex as he could get. Furthermore, it wasn't as much sex as others were having. Leonard never went to bathhouses, for instance — but mainly because he wasn't successful there. In any case, Leonard's sexuality was very spontaneous to him.

"Obviously, Leonard met a lot of men this way, but it didn't necessarily help him to find a lover. For one thing, Leonard had a tendency to be attracted to men who were not attracted to him. He went to bed with some of the most beautiful men I've ever seen, but almost without exception, he thought they went to bed with the cover of *Time* magazine, not him. He called these people 'star-fuckers,' and although he joked about it, he often felt betrayed.

"Not all of these people were 'star-fuckers,' however. Many of them genuinely admired him. He was not another notch on their belts. Still, there were very few repeats, and I think this was because even his genuine admirers were affected by the star mystique, and once that wore off, they related to him simply as a person. They did not find him physically attractive.

"Being a celebrity definitely hurt Leonard. He was disappointed repeatedly in love. Yet until the last year of his life, he gave new meaning to the phrase, 'Hope springs eternal.' The fantasy evaporated with the light of dawn over and over again, but he needed to believe, just like when he bought another Lotto ticket, that this was going to be the one. This time, he was going to win."

For some time, Matlovich's life revolved around his speaking engagements, his ongoing court battle, and his search for a lover. While his affairs still commanded the interest of the gay community, they no longer occupied page one of the national newspapers. Ever hungry for new copy, editors moved on to the Winter Olympics, the trials of Patty Hearst and Squeaky Fromme, the celebration of the U.S. Bicentennial, and the election of a new U.S. president. Along with Matlovich, the concerns of gay people quietly slipped into the national subconscious.

Nevertheless, the gay movement continued to achieve significant victories, if not in the courts, then in the city council chambers and the state houses of the nation. By January 1977, when the Dade County Commission of Miami voted five to three in favor of a major gay rights ordinance, forty other cities had done the same. In addition, according to Randy Shilts in *The Mayor of Castro Street*, nineteen states had legalized sex between consenting adults and eleven were debating gay rights bills. Furthermore, an ever-increasing number of sponsors were backing the national gay rights legislation currently before Congress.

Then a woman named Anita Bryant appeared on the scene. A former beauty queen (Miss America runner-up), entertainer ("God Bless America"), and patriot (Bob Hope Christmas tours of Vietnam), Bryant was promoting orange juice for the Florida citrus industry when the Dade County Commission passed the gay rights ordinance. Personally offended by homosexuality and outraged by the commission's action, Bryant founded Save Our Children, Inc. in protest. Within five weeks of the January commission vote, the organization had garnered six times the signatures needed to put the issue before the voters in the June election.

Gay leaders were stunned. When newspapers and magazines everywhere began featuring Bryant's picture as well as her rabid, homophobic philosophy on the front pages, they responded by organizing a national orange juice boycott. Gay people compared her to Stalin, Hitler, and the anti-Christ. Some burned her in effigy at spontaneous street demonstrations. Others assaulted her at public appearances with fruit pies. While many gay leaders worried that the confrontation was taking on the aspects of a circus sideshow, they acknowledged that the Anita Bryant affair was bringing more gay people into the movement than they had been able to do in years.

In Miami, the fight was led by Jack Campbell, the owner of Club Baths, the largest gay bathhouse chain in the nation. Along with two other activists — a woman from the Metropolitan Community Church, and "a pushy individual who wanted everything to go his own way," according to Campbell — he organized a group called the Dade County Coalition for Human Rights. When the "pushy" activist resigned as co-chair of the coalition due to differences over the orange juice boycott, Campbell asked Matlovich to fill the opening. Says Campbell:

"Even though he didn't live in Miami, we thought he would make a good spokesperson for our organization. I had met him once before, when he came to Miami to speak at a fundraiser at the Candlelight Club, and I was impressed with his ability then. He accepted our invitation and moved here for the duration. We immediately put him to work helping to raise money by speaking to political groups both in the state and across the nation."

Matlovich was not the only gay leader to get involved in the Dade County campaign. According to Shilts, "Everybody in the gay movement converged on Florida, because the movement was hitting the big time. Prior to that, only two major media stars had emerged — Lenny and Dave Kopay, the pro football player. But in Florida, the issue became bigger than any one person. That was the turning point."

One of these leaders was David Goodstein, the editor of the *Advocate*. Having met Goodstein in the course of his speaking tours, Leonard considered him a friend, but he was well aware of Goodstein's faults — in particular, his feeling that because he had a great deal of money and was the publisher the nation's biggest gay newspaper, he had the right to control things.

"I liked Goodstein because we thought a lot alike. We had the same ideas about what the movement should do to be successful. It was David's idea to hire public relations firms to advance the cause of gay liberation. He also encouraged more and more successful business people to come foward and admit that they were gay or lesbian. He wanted to work within the system and opposed more radical, confrontational tactics. He also supported the idea of marches because they were a visual show of strength — but he wanted to make the leather and drag less visible and to present a more middle-of-the-road, All-American image to the American public.

"Unfortunately, David could be abrasive. He was one of the original backers of the Gay Rights National Lobby, for instance, but when he attended the organizational meeting in Chicago, he was more or less thrown out within the first two minutes for trying to take over. 'David,' he was told, 'You bought the *Advocate* but not the movement.' They put him in his place real fast."

In Miami, Goodstein once again attempted to grab power, and this time it backfired not only on him but also on the movement, according to Matlovich.

"We desperately needed to raise money nationally, and David actually blackmailed us. He said that the only way he would assist us is if we let his management team, led by Jim Foster of San Francisco, run the campaign. The result was that we lost the election by almost a three-to-one margin. The trouble was that David's people weren't South Floridians, and they didn't understand the way things worked there. They were trying to run a big-time campaign in a small city. True, once the *Advocate* got involved, the money poured in, but they spent it as fast as it came. They squandered money left and right, just threw it away. I personally saw Jim Foster give ten thousand dollars to a black leader who promised to guarantee the black vote, but the black community voted against us overwhelmingly.

"Of course, I never thought the election should have been allowed in the first place. For about a week I kept saying, 'We really should take this to court.' I was even considering breaking away from the coalition and trying to get a lawyer to go into court to stop the election. But when you have all these high-powered people who are so experienced in the political game, you hold back because you think, 'Well, maybe they have the right answer.' But they didn't. And I think we made a major mistake there. I really think there are some things the people in this country do not have a right to vote on, and that's people's rights.

Once they are given, they should never be taken away. If in South Carolina or Georgia in the sixties whites could have voted on civil rights, blacks there still wouldn't have any civil rights at all."

According to Jack Campbell, the coalition did take the issue to court, but the court ruled against them. Furthermore, he denied that Goodstein's management team cost the coalition the election. He blamed instead the newspaper ads placed by the opposition, which likened homosexuals to child abusers and pornographers. He also felt that gay leaders were over-confident, having been misled by the polls, which gave the referendum a fifty-fifty chance of passing.

In any event, the election on June 7, 1977 was a disastrous setback for the movement, for it initiated a homophobic backlash and led to a series of similar referendums across the country. Matlovich claims he saw the writing on the wall the night before the election when he saw a mother on TV who said, "You know, I believe in civil rights for everyone, but I just don't want my child to be influenced by these people." Recalls Leonard:

"I was devastated after the election. But the night we lost, a group of us got together and led a wonderful rally in the Grand Ballroom of the Fontainbleu Hotel. We spoke to the crowd assembled there and turned the disaster into a positive thing by focusing on the good that came out of the event. We reminded the troops that there would be more battles in the future, other chances to educate people. 'We are a good and moral people,' we said, 'and we won't let them forget it.'

"At first that hotel resembled a morgue, but then people started singing and yelling, and it became a lot of fun. There was a great picture on the front page of the *Miami Herald* the next day featuring our group holding an American flag, determined to celebrate in spite of the defeat. You have to understand that we were writing the book on human sexual liberation, and we were bound to make mistakes, because no one had ever done it before."

Later that summer, Matlovich traveled to San Francisco to become involved in the city supervisor's race at the invitation of David Goodstein. Goodstein was backing a man named Rick

Stokes for supervisor in the contest for the District Five seat —
the Castro neighborhood. For the first time in the city's history,
voters there were expected to elect a gay supervisor, who would
then become the nation's highest elected gay official. Because of
this, there was considerable national interest in the election.

Rick Stokes, although a native of Oklahoma, had been active in California gay circles for a long time. He had founded the
first gay organization in Sacramento and, after moving to San
Francisco, was involved in one of the earliest gay political groups
in the country, the Society for Individual Rights. He received the
backing of Goodstein and the *Advocate* largely because his major
opponent in the race was a man named Harvey Milk, who Goodstein considered a brash, radical upstart. Notes Randy Shilts in
his biography of Milk, "To Stokes supporters, Harvey Milk was a
loudmouthed, unpredictable opportunist who had done little but
run for office since he moved to San Francisco just five years
before. To Milk supporters, Rick Stokes was just another part of
the wealthy elite, salving his wounds by kissing ass to liberal
friends."

Leonard learned a great deal about politics in San Francisco
during that campaign. He had been to San Francisco once before,
in 1975, when he ran into what he called "the political loony-
tunes" and swore he would never return. Not until the election
of 1977, however, did he realize how seriously the city took its
politics and how fragmented the gay community there had
become. Passing out literature for Stokes on the corner of Eighteenth and Castro Streets, he was often verbally assaulted by
Milk supporters who viewed him as the naive dupe of a gay
Uncle Tom. Indeed, he *was* fairly naive, for he knew nothing of
Harvey Milk and very little of Rick Stokes. Consequently, when
Milk won the election with twice as many votes as Stokes and
thirty percent of the vote in a crowded sixteen-candidate race,
Leonard failed to grasp the significance of the event. Neverthe-
less, he fell in love with the city during that visit and vowed
someday to return for a longer period of time.

The opportunity arose the following summer when John
Briggs, a conservative state senator from Orange County, California, sponsored Proposition Six, which would have barred gay

people — or anyone advocating a homosexual "lifestyle" — from teaching in the public schools. Following successive losses of gay rights referendums in Dade County, St. Paul, Wichita, and Eugene, Proposition Six was the most serious threat yet to gay civil rights and the most sweeping attack ever on the gay community. Leonard was appalled that, like Anita Bryant before him, Briggs claimed that what was at stake in California was not the civil rights of a supposedly oppressed people but the welfare of "our children" and the "moral fiber" of the country. It was a battle he could not avoid.

Months before the November election, therefore, Matlovich contacted the state offices of the No on Six campaign and offered his services. Troy Perry, the founder of the Metropolitan Community Church and the co-chair of No on Six, was delighted to hear from him. Although he had never met Leonard, he knew him by reputation, of course, and decided to put him to use the same way Jack Campbell used him in Miami, by sending him on speaking tours to raise money and support. Notes Perry:

"Everybody had told me he was a marvelous speaker, and of course he turned out to be. Since he had taught classes in the Air Force, he was used to speaking before groups of people. We criss-crossed the country together, and although Del Martin and Dave Kopay accompanied us, he and I were the major speakers. We were the ravers, as I call it. We had a real thing about emotion. He was a hard act to follow, for he was the same kind of go-for-the-gut speaker that I am. The crowd was always very responsive.

"During a tour of Texas, the largest disco in San Antonio shut down so that we could speak. Hundreds of people showed up for that. In Austin, a hundred and fifty people showed up for a dinner. In Dallas we had an overflow crowd for an auction. We also went to Houston. The whole tour was like that.

"The marvelous thing about Leonard is that he didn't even live in California at the time, but he saw the national implications. Together we told people, 'If we can't win in California, we can't win anywhere. Either we win there, or we're down the drain. There are no two ways about it.'

"Fortunately, we did win. We won partly because we were

able to get people like Leonard on board, people with national reputations and credibility who could rabble-rouse the troops. We also got people from other communities to speak out for us. It wasn't just a gay issue. In the end, we got fifty-seven percent of the total vote, over 1,300,000 more votes than the other side. Our margin of victory was nearly two to one. It was unbelievable."

Matlovich agreed and credited the win not only to gay activists and their straight friends but also to people like ex-President Ford and ex-Governor Ronald Reagan, who came out publicly against Proposition Six. When Reagan opposed Proposition Six, Leonard claimed, it became acceptable for other conservatives to do the same. Ever the conservative Republican himself, he was pleased to see the national leaders of "the party of Lincoln" refuse to duck the controversial issue, especially when leaders of the Democratic Party, like California Governor Jerry Brown and President Jimmy Carter, were hesitant to take a stand.

Shortly before the victory on Proposition Six, Matlovich was back in the public eye again — not in the news this time, but on television. On August 20, 1978, NBC aired a made-for-TV movie on "Monday Night at the Movies" titled *Sergeant Matlovich vs. the U.S. Air Force.* Starring Brad Dourif *(One Flew Over the Cuckoo's Nest)* in the title role, the movie was billed as a "moving, real life portrait of one man's courageous battle to remain in the uniform and career he so loved and respected." It ranked thirty-sixth out of fifty-nine prime time shows the week it aired and garnered twenty-five percent of the viewing audience that night — "not a particularly good rating," according to an NBC spokesperson.

Although Matlovich told an *Advocate* reporter at the time that one of the reasons for doing the film was to provide a positive role model for "gay men in Riceville, Iowa, or the lesbians in Tupelo, Mississippi," he was not pleased with the way the movie turned out. He had spent a couple of months working with the writers on the screenplay, and he felt that work on the movie was rushed and careless. Later, he spent a week with Brad Dourif, the star, so that Dourif could get to know him. But he was not called in to act as a consultant once the initial interviews were over, and he was not even allowed on the set to watch the filming.

"The first time I saw the movie was in the cutting room. I was just mortified, I thought it was so terrible. It was a disaster. It had no meat to it. I didn't like the guy who played me, for one thing. He was too meek. Naturally, I would have preferred Robert Redford or Paul Newman in the title role.

"At least the flavor was correct, even if the facts weren't quite right. You have to realize that a lot of the characters in the movie were composites. One character represented five or six different people in my life. The thing that upset me the most, though, was the scene where a straight friend comes in and prevents me from committing suicide. That simply wasn't true. I argued with the producer about that. *I* was the one who stopped myself, I said. No straight person prevented me from doing that. He said he wanted to show the compassion that straights can have for gays. But I pointed out that all he did was reinforce the image of gay people as mealy-mouthed, weak-livered cowards.

"But I guess it was important in some respects. It was one of the first gay movies. And I know it's done a lot of good, for I've had countless phone calls as a result. A friend of mine told me that he and his father broke off their relationship twenty years ago, and his father happened one night to watch that movie. As a result, his father called him, and they got back together again. In my own family it did some good, too. When the movie appeared on TV, I watched it with my parents up in Wisconsin at my sister's house. Their reaction was very positive. My father cried during the father-son scene. But I separated myself from all that. It was too strange, seeing myself being portrayed on screen."

The same day *Sergeant Matlovich vs. the U.S. Air Force* aired on TV, the Defense Department announced that veterans of military service, including homosexuals, could apply for an upgraded discharge based on their service record. This applied to administrative discharges only, not to those based on misconduct. Still, it was a "dramatic change," according to an *Advocate* reporter, who attributed it, in large part, to Leonard's 1976 court battle.

On December 6, 1978, that battle finally reached another plateau with a unanimous decision by the United States Court of Appeals for the District of Columbia to overturn the lower court rulings discharging both Sergeant Matlovich and Ensign Berg from the Armed Services. For Leonard, it was the first victory in a 3½-year campaign, and he was elated. The decision did not mean that he was to be reinstated in the Air Force, however. Instead, the Court of Appeals sent the case back to Judge Gesell of the United States District Court, who was instructed to order the Air Force to come up with new guidelines for their exception policy. As David Addlestone, who was no longer directly involved with the case, explains:

"The panel didn't even touch the constitutional issue, which had been pursued despite the Supreme Court's refusal to hear the Virginia sodomy case. They decided on very narrow administrative law grounds instead. They said, 'Look, the Air Force claims they've got an exception to the policy. They've got to state some reason why they're kicking him out. Either they must exclude everybody or come up with some standards stating how they decide who they are going to keep.' The Air Force, who by this time had made three or four different representations as to what their policy was, kept insisting that they had the right to be totally arbitrary. If they wanted to keep a gay person in, they'd know it when they saw it, they said. The Court of Appeals refused to accept that. So they sent it back to Gesell. By forcing the Air Force to adopt exception guidelines, the Court was essentially buying my back-up position — if you can't get them on the constitutional issue, get them on their own territory."

Carrington Boggan, who presented the case to the Court of Appeals, said essentially the same thing:

"Our primary goal was to have the military's policy thrown out as unconstitutional. My view was that since the Supreme Court had not definitively stated any reasons for their Virginia sodomy ruling, it was still an open issue. But the Court of Appeals said it wasn't necessary for them to decide on that basis, since it could resolve the case on an administrative law basis instead. That is typical of how a court will approach a constitutional issue.

"Therefore we argued that the Air Force's exception policy was itself an exception, a matter of personal whim and discretion by individual commanding officers acting in a completely arbitrary and capricious manner. The Court agreed that the Air Force had no clear standards or guidelines as to what would constitute an exception. The Court therefore had no basis on which to review the Air Force's policy concerning the exclusion of homosexuals. So it reversed the lower court ruling and said that the case would have to go back to the Air Force to clarify. The Air Force could then have asked the Supreme Court to grant review, but they chose not to do so. They chose instead to try to comply with the Court of Appeals decision."

Concluded the *Advocate*, "The court decision throws the burden of proof back to the Armed Forces, where the drawing up of guidelines for expulsion of homosexuals might take years." Having fought this long, Matlovich was prepared to wait.

7

The Move West

In March of 1979, Leonard fulfilled a promise to himself and moved from Washington to San Francisco, the city he had fallen in love with the year before. He arrived there less than four months after the assassinations of Mayor George Moscone and Supervisor Harvey Milk by Supervisor Dan White — assassinations which rocked the city and the nation. Although Matlovich had campaigned against Milk during the 1977 elections, he claimed that in time he grew to admire the man who was destined to become the the gay movement's most important martyr.

"The first time I met Milk, I was passing out literature to the crowd by Twin Peaks bar at the corner of Castro and Market. Milk walked by and said, 'Matlovich, you son-of-a-bitch carpetbagger, get out of this city.' Since he was the political opposition, that just reinforced my negative feelings about him. Later, however, my feelings changed. About a month before he was murdered, he and I were on a gay rights panel discussion, and I was very impressed with him. I made up my mind then that I was going to take him up on his offer to have lunch together someday. I really think that had Milk lived, we would probably have become political allies. We had different styles, but in the long run, we cared about the same things." Although Matlovich missed the candlelight march for the city's abrasive yet well-loved gay supervisor immediately following the assassinations, he did witness the event's dramatic aftermath. On the night of May 21, 1979, hours after a jury convicted killer Dan White of voluntary manslaughter rather than first-degree murder, thousands of protestors, gay and straight, took to the streets in anger. Led by a young street activist named Cleve Jones, they spontaneously marched from Castro Street down Market toward City Hall, where their anger erupted in violence. Undeterred by pleas from community leaders for restraint, the crowd swept past police barricades, smashed every window on the first floor of City Hall, and set fire to rows of police cars. Worse was to follow when the police, bent on revenge, invaded the Castro, stormed a gay bar named the Elephant Walk, and attacked every "cock-sucker" in sight later the same night. Leonard saw it all.

"My friend Michael Bedwell [who joined Leonard in San Francisco as his roommate in early 1979] and I were down on the steps of City Hall trying to stop the mob action. We had formed a human chain across the doors to prevent people from damaging the building. Obviously, we didn't do much good. I remember seeing Cleve Jones trying to calm the crowd and Supervisor Carol Ruth Silver getting hit in the face with a brick. I was hit pretty hard in the face myself. People next to me were ripping the grillwork from the front of City Hall and using it to batter the windows in. Others were setting police cars on fire while the police stood by and watched their cars burn. It was incredible. I had never seen anything like this before. Michael and I stayed until the cars were burning, probably eleven or twelve o'clock. Then we returned to my apartment at the corner of Castro and Eighteenth Streets.

"When we arrived, two police ambulances were parked in the middle of the street near a group of people singing, 'Happy Birthday, Harvey Milk' (whose birthday would have been the next day). Across the way, over at the Elephant Walk, a crowd of people was taunting a line of police. Someone in the crowd threw something at the police — a drink or a can of beer or something. The police line broke and fell back. Then it went charging forward into the Elephant Walk, where the police battered the shit out of the bar and the people inside.

"As people fled screaming and bleeding from the bar, some were taken inside the police ambulances, where they were administered first aid. All the while, police in military formation were marching down the middle of the street shouting in cadence, 'Hup, two, three, hup, two, three' while on the sidewalk gay people continued to sing, 'Happy Birthday, Harvey Milk.' We watched all this from the roof of my building, and it was incredible.

"I had very mixed feelings about what was going on. I thought the anger was just anger. I, too, was angry that a man was getting away with murder, and I was glad that we were fighting back. We were showing them that we weren't the pansies they always thought we were. But politically it was a setback. Violence is always a setback. It means that communication has broken down. Besides, for so long, everywhere I spoke, I said that we as gay and lesbian people were teaching people to love — not to hate — and I felt that our anger was out of character with what I had been preaching for so many years."

For Matlovich, the event had one unexpected but humorous consequence. About six months after the "White Night Riots," the FBI paid him a visit. The bureau was investigating alleged violations of citizens' rights by the San Francisco Police Department, and as part of its investigation, it was seeking statements from witnesses. To give the visiting agents a clearer picture of what he had seen, Leonard escorted the agents to the roof, where a neighbor was growing marjuana on the fire escape. Matlovich didn't even notice the plants, but the agent interrupted his account of the police riots to ask, "Is that your marijuana?" Leonard replied, "God no!" and called his neighbors as soon as the agent left to warn them to get rid of the illegal weed before they, too, received a visit from the FBI. Fortunately, the FBI had other fish to fry that day, and the neighbors never did hear from Leonard's visitors.

Following this dramatic introduction to life in San Francisco, Matlovich kept his eyes open. With one eye, he looked for a suitable place for himself in the Byzantine labyrinth of local gay politics. With the other, he continued his lifelong search for a lover. True to form, he was still looking for "Mr. Wonderful," and he thought that among the many thousands of gay men in San Francisco, he was bound to find one who was perfect — or nearly so.

Surprisingly, he did meet someone fairly quickly — but not in San Francisco. When he was in Chicago speaking before a Metropolitan Community Church congregation, a man in the audience caught his eye. Leonard asked him out for a date afterward and immediately fell "head over heels" in love. The man turned out to be a wholesale jewelry salesman named Tom, ten years younger than him, who was more than willing to return Leonard's affection. That first date was such a success that as soon as Leonard returned to San Francisco, Tom followed to visit. It was the beginning of a relationship that, for a while at least, helped to keep the airlines in business.

"I was doing a lot of traveling then, and I would always route myself through Chicago in order to spend time with him. We dated for about a year altogether, but it was hard because it was a long-distance relationship. Nevertheless, he meant a lot to me — so much that I was willing to jeopardize my relationship with my parents for his sake. When I told my parents we were dating, my mother said, 'Well, don't bring him home.' And I said, 'Then you'll never see me again,' and I hung up the phone. She immediately called me back and said that he could come after all. I was determined that if he wasn't welcome in their house, then neither was I.

"In any event, it never came to that. Before I had a chance to introduce him to my parents, we broke up over the stupidest thing — cigarettes. When I first met Tom, he quit smoking for my sake. That was a very powerful thing for me — that he cared enough to give up cigarettes. But then he started smoking again due to difficulty at work, and I thought it was because he didn't care about me any more. Because of that, I destroyed the relationship. In retropect, that seems terribly silly. Had I been more mature, we would probably still be happily in love, and I'd be living in Chicago today. Who knows?"

Michael Bedwell remembers the affair differently:

"Leonard had two types. One was the stereotypical clone. For years he had this painting in his room of a sailor who represented this type — a big muscular guy with dark hair, a bushy mustache, and a huge cock. It was tacky gay art, but Leonard thought it was wonderful. The other was the teddy bear, slightly smaller and chunky. Tom was one of the latter. I only met him once or twice, since he lived in Chicago, but I heard enough about the relationship through Leonard to know that cigarettes were just an excuse Leonard used to mask Tom's declining affection. When they broke up, Leonard admitted that it was because Tom simply wasn't interested in him any more.

"On the surface, Leonard accepted the fact fairly quickly, but it took him a long time to get over the pain. That's one of the reasons he seemed so defensive about it in retrospect. Quite frankly, I didn't think Tommy was good enough for Leonard. I thought he was an airhead, a cipher. In any case, I doubt whether anything Leonard could have done would have affected the outcome of the relationship one way or the other. It was over."

The relationship with Tom at an end, Leonard compensated for the lack of love by devoting his energies to politics instead. First he joined the Concerned Republicans for Individual Rights, a gay group. Then he decided to challenge Harry Britt, the man who replaced Harvey Milk, for the seat from District Five in the November 1979 supervisors' race.

For Matlovich, returning to the Republican party after registering as a Democrat in Washington, D.C. was like coming home after years in the wilderness.

"When you live in Washington, it's so heavily Democratic that if you belong to any other party you just don't count. So my friends there convinced me to join their party. But I was like a fish out of water as a Democrat. I felt more at home in the Republican Party, because those were my roots.

"Sometimes, as a gay person in a party which is socially as well as politically conservative, I do wonder if I'm not the good Jew inviting the Gestapo over for ham. But the reality is that we're a two-party system in this country, and we ought to be able to join whatever party we want, whether we are gay or not. Unfortunately, twenty years ago, when gays in the Democratic

Party were changing attitudes within the party, gays in the Republican party weren't doing the same thing. Therefore, as far as gay rights issues are concerned, the Republican party is far behind. But I simply refuse to give up the party of Lincoln to the bigots.

"The trouble is that after Goldwater was defeated, vacuums were created within the Republican party that all the old Dixiecrats and disaffected Southern Democrats took over — people like Jesse Helms of North Carolina. Perhaps it's too late to do anything about people like Helms, but it's not too late to influence other Republicans. I'm going to be there educating them. I know that most Republicans don't have a very good track record on gay rights, but I believe that some day the Republican Party will come around, absolutely. Otherwise, what's the alternative? To put all our eggs in one basket, the Democrats'? Then when those eggs break, where do we turn?

"We have to understand that gay and lesbian unity doesn't mean gay and lesbian uniformity. We have a much better chance of success when we allow the left of the movement and the right of the movement an equal voice in community affairs. We need to move foward, yet we spend so much time criticizing each other. As long as that happens, we will not be free."

Due to his political conservatism and his past military history, Leonard was not immediately understood or accepted by the vast majority of San Francisco gay activists, most of whom belonged to what he continued to call "the loony left." Many regarded him as an interloper in community affairs — a "carpetbagger," according to Harvey Milk. Therefore, they resented his decision to run in the 1979 supervisor's race against Harry Britt, Milk's chosen successor.

Although new to the city, Matlovich did the best he could to organize some kind of support. He directed his appeal toward fellow conservatives and "moderate" Democrats. Ten or fifteen people helped with his campaign and managed to raise several thousand dollars. Most of the money was raised through a mailer sent to the names on a donors' list obtained at City Hall. He also sought endorsements from established business groups such as the Board of Realtors.

But all was to no avail. His name was familiar to the voters of District Five, but his message fell on deaf ears. In a crowded field of twelve candidates, half of whom were gay, Matlovich placed seventh, garnering just 410 votes — two percent of the total. The top finisher, with twenty-seven percent of the vote, was Harry Britt, who eventually won a run-off election against the first runner-up, a straight, liberal attorney named Terrance Hallinan. Milk's legacy, Leonard learned, combined with his own inexperience, was an unsurmountable obstacle.

"Being very naive, I thought I could win, so I ran hard. The writing was on the wall, but I just didn't see it. I was too conservative, and that was that. Besides, I had the misconception that I could just move in and run on the strength of my name alone. You can't do things like that, especially in a neighborhood city like San Francisco. You need organization, you need money, and you have to pay your dues.

"I ran mainly because my entire life I've been interested in politics, and I've always had a desire to run for public office. By running, I settled that desire. I don't regret running, of course. But I don't think I mind having lost either, because I've come to the conclusion that when you are elected to public office, to some degree you lose your ability to be objective. All of a sudden you have to start paying the piper — or the masses — and you can no longer say what you believe without having to worry about the political ramifications."

While Matlovich attributed his disappointing showing in the supervisor's race to several factors — his lack of organization, financial backing, and experience; the martyred Milk's mantle; and his own conservatism — most of his friends and opponents focused on the last issue. It was Leonard's political conservatism, they said, which made it impossible for him to win election in San Francisco. Even though they agreed with him that "gay and lesbian unity doesn't mean gay and lesbian uniformity," most gay people simply could not bring themselves to vote for a man who took pride in being a Republican. Said Frank Kameny:

"With all due respect, Leonard's politics were and are conservative in ways that did not get him the following of large segments of the gay community. He was not, although he tried to be, the kind of charismatic leader that one might have needed. His heart was in the right place, but his politics were not. Consequently, he didn't do terribly well in his political endeavors in San Francisco. He did serve, along with some others, to bring together something of a Republican presence within the gay movement and of gays within the Republican party that has been useful to some extent. Unfortunately, that effort didn't go as far as it might have. I am very much a Democrat, but I do feel we need to be everywhere in every way."

However, others disagreed. Unlike Kameny, Troy Perry, for one, downplayed the significance of Matlovich's political beliefs:

"Some people think that if you're gay, you automatically have to be a liberal Democrat bordering on a socialist, but that's just not true. I've learned over the years that we're all kinds of people and that we reflect the general population, no more, no less. Leonard, for instance, is a conservative Republican and I'm a liberal Democrat, but we've never let that personally get in our way. We have never gotten into an argument over that or any other issue. True, he's been controversial, but I think he and I get along real well."

"Getting along real well," however, does not guarantee success at the polls. As far as most gay people were concerned at the time, and as Frank Kameny implied, there was a "right place" to be in the political spectrum. Perhaps it was not necessary for all gay people to be "liberal Democrats bordering on socialists," but that *was* necessary for gay candidates who wanted to win elections — a lesson that was not lost on Leonard.

After the election, Matlovich realized that it was time to settle down and find a job. His star was fading, and he was no longer able to survive on income from speaking engagements and public appearances. He had not held a "real job" since leaving the Air Force in 1976, and he was getting tired of leading a life of poverty. He found a job by walking door to door down Eighteenth Street, covering first one side of the street and then the other, offering his services to anyone who could use them — in whatever capacity.

On Sixteenth Street, a company named Dillon Tile, which sold tiles to building contractors, happened to have an opening for a warehouseman. The manager, impressed by Matlovich's earnest and eager manner, hired him on the spot, even though Leonard admitted he knew nothing about the business. Later, when one owner of the old family-run business reviewed Leonard's application, he immediately recognized the name and said to his manager, "Oh my God, what have you done? You've hired a gay radical!" He stuck by the manager's decision, however, and he soon discovered that Leonard was a valuable employee, "radical" or not.

As a warehouseman, Matlovich made $4.25 an hour six days a week, mainly filling orders. He also worked a lot of overtime. He was hardly rich, but he made enough to pay his rent and to finance his continuing search for Mr. Right at area gay bars. He directed most of his energies, however, not to his social life but to his job. As a result, he was promoted after six months to warehouse manager and his salary was doubled. His responsibilities as manager included every aspect of warehouse operation.

While the warehouse job was a far cry from the kind of work he was doing for the Air Force when he was discharged, Leonard enjoyed it. He especially enjoyed the opportunity to change the stereotypes of gay people held by so many of the "macho, redneck types" who came in to place orders with him. Most knew who he was, and many, after seeing his name in the newspaper or his face on TV, would say to him, "Hey, I heard what you said last night. You were pretty good."

Matlovich's co-workers and customers were soon to see a great deal more of him in the news, for on September 9, 1980, Judge Gerhard Gesell, to whom the Court of Appeals had remanded Leonard's case two years earlier, finally issued a decision regarding the case. Ruling that the Air Force had refused to comply with the Court of Appeals' demand for a clarification of the exception policy, he ordered Matlovich back into the Air Force at full rank with back pay. According to Matlovich's lawyer, Carrington Boggan:

"From 1978 to 1980 the Air Force tried to come up with a basis which would justify its actions in the form of a clarification of its policy. They filed what was called a 'declaration' with Gesell, which was an attempt to explain how they proceeded. But it really did not clarify anything. It did not give any guidelines which would be generally applicable to deciding similar cases, and that's why Gesell rejected it.

"In the meantime, the Air Force also changed its policy to eliminate the exception provision that had gotten them in so much trouble. Under the new policy, there was no longer any basis for retaining people on exceptional grounds. But because Matlovich was discharged before they changed their policy, the rule that was applicable to him was the one in effect at that time, and they still had to try to answer the court's objection to that."

As usual, David Addlestone's interpretation of the affair was more blunt than that of Boggan. Recognizing that Leonard could still win the case on narrow grounds after the Court of Appeals victory in 1978, Addlestone reversed his previous decision to withdraw from the case and decided that such a victory would be better than nothing. Therefore, he offered Matlovich his help for free once again, and he worked with Boggan on the case Recalls Addlestone:

"Basically, what happened was every time a new Secretary of the Air Force was appointed, the Air Force filed some new affidavit in the court that was slightly different from the last one. Since the policy kept changing all the time, Gesell got very angry. He is a judge to be feared, and he really projected his anger to the government. I think he knew that they didn't have the guts to appeal the case.

"It was pretty clear that the Justice Department lawyers were embarrassed to be in court with what they had. A lot of what goes on in court is a matter of perception, and I think the government said to him, 'Judge, we really stepped on our dicks in this case, and we're going to do everything we can to keep it away from the circuit.' Gesell picked up on those undercurrents and rammed it to them. It was devastating.

"So Gesell ruled in Matt's favor on the narrow grounds. He instructed the Air Force to put Matt back in the service, promote him, and void his bar to re-enlistment. He went all the way, which is further than I had ever seen any other judge do. I think the reason was that basically the Air Force had misrepresented their policy to the court, and he made them regret it."

At that point, the Air Force could have appealed Gesell's decision, but it chose instead to propose settlement talks with Matlovich. Leonard himself could not appeal, since the judge ordered him back in. With the constitutional argument dead in the water, he had either to re-enlist or accept a financial settlement. After conferring with Boggan and Addlestone, he chose to enter into settlement discussions. Because this called for an extensive amount of factual record development, which his lawyers were not equipped to handle, they called in Wilmer, Cutler and Pickering, a major Washington D.C. law firm, to assist.

According to Addlestone, the Air Force authorities made their offer to Matlovich based on actuarial grounds. They figured out what his back pay, his years of future service, and his pension would be worth if he were reinstated. Then they made him an offer of $160,000 — which, since the offer was couched in terms of constitutional damages, was tax-free. Says Addlestone.

"The Air Force brass made it clear that they did not want him to put the uniform on. They really bent over backwards to avoid that, and they were willing to pay dearly for it. The alternative was for him to go back on active duty, put on the uniform, and have them throw him back out as soon as possible on some trumped-up charges. And this time, they wouldn't screw around like they did the last time by giving us a forum. Before, they really got suckered in, because we caught them trying to do some really nasty things, things that all my life I wanted to expose but didn't in exchange for the media show they gave us and Matt's cause.

"In any event, once the Air Force made the offer, it was Matt's decision whether or not to accept. My advice was, 'Walk away a winner. Put the money to good use.' He'd been out as a civilian for four years. They would have made him miserable if he had been back in the Air Force. This way, he could come out proclaiming victory over a severely embarrassed Air Force and get on with his life.

"A lot of people were very adamant that he should go back

in, fall down on his sword, and give up the money. It was easy for them to say, 'Chief, why don't you give up $160,000 tax-free and go back in and carry on the cause?' So what that he'd be discharged with nothing in the long run? They didn't have to make the sacrifice. He did."

Turning to friends as well as to his lawyers for advice, Leonard eventually decided that Addlestone's arguments were sound ones and he accepted the money — a decision he later called the hardest of his life.

"Everyone agreed that if the Air Force took me back they'd throw me right out again under the new regulations, which were established when they dropped the exception clause. Even if they didn't, they would get me on something else. Now I'm not stupid. I was in the military long enough to know that the Air Force would find a way to make the threats of my former first sergeant come true. And I didn't want that to happen. I wanted to fight for gay and lesbian rights, but I didn't want to be a martyr. None of my heroes have been martyrs. General Patton said that no poor dumb bastard ever won a war by dying for his country. He won the war by making the other poor dumb bastard die for his country.

"Some people accused me of selling out when I took the money, but I didn't see it that way. Even if I could have continued the fight, what was the point? It wasn't a constitutional case any more, and there was nothing I could do about that. Things had progressed beyond my control. So how was I selling out? By not going back in to prove a point? I had already proved the point. No, from my point of view it was a victory, for I showed that you *can* take on the military and win. You might not get what you're after, but you can at least get back pay and a promotion, or, if it is offered, settlement money."

Matlovich's lawyers agreed that the settlement was a victory for him personally as well as for the gay community — but it was a limited one. Said Patricia Douglass, the attorney who handled the case for Wilmer and Pickering:

"There's no question that it was a victory. It would have been very nice to get a constitutional ruling, but that just wasn't the posture of the case. When you're a lawyer, you have to look at the case you have. You don't often get a hypothetical, theoretical policy issue."

Agreed Carrington Boggan: "It was a victory in the sense that the military was recognizing that they had a serious problem with their policy, one they were not willing to subject to the challenge of further litigation. Of course, it was not the victory we had wanted, which was a declaration by a court that their policy was invalid. But in litigation you almost never get exactly what you want. The court will usually find some basis for acting that's not precisely what you had hoped for. Nevertheless, the decision by the Court of Appeals made clear that the services were proceeding on an irrational basis, one that could not even be reviewed by the Court. The services, in deciding to settle, were in effect admitting that they had a problem with the application of their policies. At that point they were not willing to take a chance on what a higher court would say."

David Addlestone was equally satisfied with the outcome of the case, but for reasons which pleased him as a social reformer as well as a lawyer:

"It was a victory because it changed the popular image of gays. It brought people out of the closet who were in positions of authority in the Air Force. It affected the way the V.A. treated people with undesirable discharges for homosexuality. And it forced the services to change their regulations as to what types of discharges they were giving people who committed homosexual acts. All of this flowed from the case. But it did, in fact, solidify the military's attitude and led them to formulate an absolute policy barring gays. Frankly, I don't think they would have done this otherwise."

For this last reason, Frank Kameny, the gay rights activist who first advised Matlovich about challenging the Air Force, did not agree with Leonard's lawyers that the case was a success:

"Certainly, Matlovich didn't win. The military eventually proved to be unreformable. The worst elements remained in control, the neanderthals. Following the case, they rewrote their policy and came out with rigorous, airtight regulations which put into effect a total, unbending and inflexible exclusion of all homosexuals.

"Nevertheless, I don't regret having challenged the military. If it hadn't been Matlovich, it would have been somebody else. The change was in the air, and his was as perfect a challenge as we could ever have expected to have. In general, challenges are important even if you fail. Obviously, you have to examine the particular issue and situation. Your decision has to be made *ad hoc* in these kinds of things. You are acting dangerously if you act wholely on the basis of broad, overarching principles. But in general, yes, these things must be challenged."

Whether or not they agreed that the case was a success, Matlovich and his advisors agreed on one thing — the case did nothing to enlighten the military's attitude toward homosexuals. According to Hans Mark, the Secretary of the Air Force at the time, the settlement with Matlovich was devised "because we continue to regard homosexuality as fundamentally inconsistent with military service and wanted to avoid returning [him] to active duty." Michael Clark, the executive director of San Franciso's Gay Rights Advocates, surely recognized this when, speaking for the gay community, he vowed that the fight against the military would continue. Said Clark, the settlement was "very favorable for us. . . . The appellate decision is left standing, so we can base further litigation on it."

As far as Leonard was concerned, the case was finally over. But for the gay community, much more would follow.

8

Back to Business

Matlovich found several uses for the money he received from the Air Force. Some he gave to the Gay Men's Chorus of San Francisco, which was planning its first national tour. A portion he donated to gay and lesbian business and professional organizations. But the bulk of it he devoted to his own private project. After quitting his warehouse job, he opened a pizza parlor named Stumptown Annie's in the Russian River resort town of Guerneville, California, sixty miles north of San Francisco.

Although he had never owned a business before, Leonard was at least familiar with the town he intended to make his home. He first visited Guerneville in the early 1960s, as a young airman stationed at Travis Air Force Base. On weekends, he and a group of fellow servicemen would travel all over Northern California, and the quaint Russian River community was one of their favorite destinations.

Guerneville had been a quiet place then, nestled amid the redwoods and vineyards of the coastal range a few miles from the Pacific. Visitors — mostly families from San Francisco and its suburbs — came to enjoy the beautiful scenery, the warm summer weather, and the slow pace of the small town. Fishing on the river's placid waters, swimming at rocky Johnson's Beach, or browsing at the Five and Dime on Main Street was just about all the town could offer in the way of excitement.

In the late 1970s, however, the situation changed drastically. Many of the gay men and women who had moved to San Francisco by the thousands a few years earlier soon grew tired of the frenzied lifestyles they led in the city and discovered in Guerneville the ideal retreat. Joining counter-cultural predecessors who led the way "back to nature" in the mid-sixties, they bought homes and opened businesses in and around the town whose name newcomers invariably mangled. Other gay people, delighted to find an oasis in the country where they could express themselves openly, came up for extended weekends in the summer. Before long, there were so many gay migrants to the area — residents and visitors alike — that Guerneville gained a reputation as a gay resort town.

In some ways this was self-defeating, for, as more and more gay people moved into the area, "The River" soon began to resemble the gay ghettos they were trying to escape (if only temporarily). At all-night discos, for instance, gay people could party the night away, choose a partner from an inexhaustible supply of possibilities, and sleep until afternoon the following day, just as so many did in San Francisco. But at the river, at least, other options existed, and people like Leonard Matlovich were quick to take advantage of them.

For Matlovich, the opportunity to become financially independent in an environment more conducive to his own mainstream temperament was a dream come true. Although he regretted leaving behind the fractious and exciting world of San Francisco gay politics, Guerneville offered compensations which appealed to him far more.

"I love the country. And I've always loved Guerneville since the first time I visited. It's so picturesque. Moving there was the fulfillment of a fantasy, for I was able to have the country, the companionship of other gay people, and my own business all at the same time.

"Getting the restaurant off the ground, however, was a lot harder than I thought it would be. Because Guerneville didn't even have a pizza place at the time, it seemed like a sure bet. So I checked around and found the perfect location, right on Main Street at the busiest intersection in town. Just to get the permit to open the place proved to be a nightmare, however. The previous business in that location had been a health food store, and when the owners sold it to me, they sold it as a restaurant. Transferring the old license to my new business would be just a formality, I thought. But the local officials didn't see it that way.

"Because the town was on a septic system rather than a sewage system, the Water Resource Control Board wasn't allowing any new restaurants to open — the system couldn't handle it — and they considered my restaurant a new one. Luckily, in spite of government bureaucracy, I managed to get it through somehow. Still, I was required to use paper plates and plastic silverware as a water-saving device, and that ate up a lot of the profits. I was also required to monitor how much water I used each month, so I didn't use more than I had used the month before. That was a great inconvenience for me.

"In fact, the only time I ever threw a customer out was when he complained about the paper plates and claimed that I was too cheap to buy the real thing. I tried to explain to him that by law I was not allowed to have a dishwasher, and I tried to have high-quality paper instead, but he wouldn't listen. He called me a liar, so I got rid of him — quick."

Difficulties with the Water Resource Control Board and with petulant customers were not the only problems Matlovich faced in opening his new restaurant. Notes Michael Bedwell:

"When Leonard opened Stumptown Annie's, I moved to Guerneville to help him manage. He neglected to tell me, however, that he had asked someone else to manage as well. It's a classic Leonard story — not being able to say no. Leonard didn't have the heart to choose only one of us.

"It turned out to be a nightmare. Fortunately, I had kept my apartment in San Francisco in case things didn't work out — and they didn't. A month later, we had one of our famous arguments, so I quit and turned the place over to the other manager. Leonard and I didn't talk again for three months. Then he called me or I called him, and it was as if it had never happened. In the mean-

time, the other manager lasted until Leonard caught him steal-
ing money to pay for cocaine."

Temporary battles with Bedwell aside, the residents of
Guerneville were keenly interested in the man who ran the new
pizza parlor. According to Steve Pizzo, the former co-publisher
of the *Russian River News*, Leonard's appearance in Guerneville
created quite a stir, at least at the beginning.

"Residents of this rural country town were a little nervous
about gay people taking over in those days, for we were experiencing a major demographic change. The biggest move prior to
that was when a gay man bought Fife's, the largest resort complex in the area. But this is a fairly resilient little town, and the
people who lived here were beginning to get used to the changes
taking place. Still, when Leonard opened up his pizza place, it
was new, it was the talk of the town, and people were watching
to see what would happen.

"When Leonard first arrived, we all trudged over to meet
him. We were greeted with this ever-happy, ever-smiling, ever-
animated, never-at-a-loss-for-words character who had a huge
picture of Barry Goldwater hanging up in his restaurant with the
words inscribed, 'In your heart you know he's right.' I kept trying
to fathom what this was all about. I knew this man had stood up
against the Air Force before anybody else had dared to do so, and I
knew that he had made the cover of *Time* as a result. But having
a picture of a right-wing Republican hanging in his restaurant
just didn't jive.

"As the years went by, though, I got to know Leonard well,
and I learned that he didn't fit any particular stereotype. Leonard
was Leonard. What you saw was what you got. He was always
right out there with his opinions, and he didn't care what other
people thought. He became one of my favorite people."

Matlovich wasted no time adapting himself to the life of a
small-town businessman. His primary concern was to turn a
profit, which he did after the first year. He didn't turn a profit
earlier, he claims, because he put "every dime" he made back
into the restaurant to make it successful. Since he had no previous experience in the restaurant business, it took him a while to

figure out what he was doing. Among other things, he learned that in a resort community like Guerneville, the amount of business varies radically from summer to winter. He managed to stay open year-round by cutting back in the winter and reducing his staff from from a high of thirty to a low of seven. The rest of what he learned came as a result of three years, "almost to the day," he recalled, "of hard, hard work."

While Leonard was primarily concerned with establishing a successful business, he was equally concerned with becoming a valued member of the community. He joined a bevy of organizations — the Chamber of Commerce Board of Directors, the River Community Services Board of Directors, the Russian River Republican Club, the Sonoma County Republican Central Committee, and others. He also gave donations and free meals to various causes. One example was the one thousand dollars worth of savings bonds he gave to the winners of a local grammar school essay contest. He did all this not only because it was natural for him to become involved in community affairs; it was also good for business.

As a result, he earned the respect and appreciation of fellow businessmen and ordinary citizens in Guerneville. At the same time, however, he managed to create the same kind of controversy that he had in San Francisco — not because his political and professional commitments were too conservative or too liberal, but simply because he was so outspoken about whatever cause or position he was promoting at the time. According to Steve Pizzo:

"He was very vocal. Leonard always had an opinion on anything that was going on. We were constantly interviewing him for the paper, and he was constantly pushing one or another of his favorite projects. Town beautification was one of these. He was dead-set on getting this town cleaned up, and he made some headway along that line, but not without ruffling a few feathers along the way.

"He was also concerned with gay-straight relations in this town. I remember once he came flying over to our office completely upset. Now, when Leonard gets upset, his face turns red, he starts talking very quickly, and he flails the air with those spaghetti arms of his. Anyway, he was screaming and yelling, and I said, 'Leonard, what is the problem?' He replied, 'High school kids are sitting on the bench in front of my restaurant and yelling "Faggot!" at people as they go by!' I tried to calm him down and said, 'Oh Leonard, gay people from the city are mature enough to know that those are just high school kids who don't know any better.' Leonard concluded, 'Yeah, but that's not the problem. The problem is that they're yelling at straight people!'"

Pizzo's partner at the *Russian River News*, editor Scott Kersnar, was also well-acquainted with Matlovich's passionate but controversial behavior. Recalls Kersnar:

"Leonard was well-liked in the community, but he was also resented by some people. Once, for instance, he brought the San Francisco Lesbian and Gay Freedom Day Marching Band to a Chamber of Commerce awards banquet held at Buck's, an Italian restaurant that usually featured country and western music. That might have gone over all right if he had discussed it with people in advance, but because he thought the idea might be opposed by the usual customers at Buck's, he sprang it on us as a surprise. It created quite a stir. Some people grumbled and didn't think it was at all funny.

"Straight people weren't the only ones Leonard offended. There were a number of gay business leaders as well who sometimes wished that Leonard would just shut up. The president of the Chamber of Commerce at that time was gay, but he didn't always know what Leonard was going to do either. People who weren't as flamboyant as Leonard found him a bit much.

"But what they didn't understand is that Leonard is Leonard wherever he is. He does not avoid the public spotlight. He's very stubborn and unwilling to give up or to compromise on the issues that are important to him. For a lot of people, that's abrasive, but for others, that's what they love about the guy. He's irrepressible, incorrigible."

Michael Bedwell agrees:

"When Leonard had a hair up his ass about something, there were no mountains or walls high enough to prevent him from charging foward. He had a tendency to fly off the handle. He might regret it later and apologize, but that didn't mean the same thing wouldn't happen again the next time. Although we were as close to one another as we could be without being lovers, we had some severe fights. The fight concerning the restaurant in Guerneville was one of those. Another centered around a house guest, as so many did. But that particular fight led to a dent in my kitchen wall which is still there.

"Leonard was such a seemingly-contradictory combination of things. On the one hand, he was so gentle and childlike. He got into trouble repeatedly by wanting to avoid conflict with people, by wanting everyone to like him. But on the other hand, he was stubborn and irrational. He had a deep-seated anger and rage that, when brought to the surface, often caused him no end of trouble. When he allowed that anger to take control, he was like a bull in a china shop."

Continues Kersnar:

"One of the things Leonard was very proud of was erecting a flagpole on the corner in front of his pizza parlor and running the flag up every day. When he was in town last, the first thing he said to me was, 'Why isn't the flag up? The person who is in charge of it now should have the flag up every day.' The flagpole is one of the things Leonard was most associated with in this town, far more than controversial affairs like the event at Buck's.

"In many ways, Leonard fit into life here well, for this town has always attracted people with a flair, people who want for one reason or another to reside in a live-and-let-live community. It's a very cause-oriented place. People care passionately about their own beliefs and are always ready to run off in every direction, but at the same time, they are proud of the town's oddball flavor."

Like Kersnar, Matlovich took great pride in the tolerance of Guerneville's citizens.

"Guerneville is an enchanted town, because it has people from the far left to the far right, and they somehow manage to get along. It was so fabulous to live there, especially in the wintertime, for it was then that we were closest as a community. I used to get rushes, thrills, when gay couples, straight couples, and a couple of kids would all mix in the restaurant. It was just wonderful. I mean, there were some real rednecks who ate there.

Some even gave me gifts because of the things I did. Like I've said before, I believe in flaunting your virtues. If you do, it pays off — for everyone."

Even Matlovich, however, acknowledged that there were drawbacks to living in the isolated Russian River town. One of these was loneliness. It was one of the main reasons he worked so hard to make his restaurant a success, for, by pouring his energies into the business, he kept his mind off other things. But loneliness did not last forever. On a trip to Los Angeles one weekend, Leonard was speaking before the gay Catholic group, Dignity, when he met an insurance underwriter named Jeff. Jeff became the next in a long line of Matlovich boyfriends, but the first who taught him "that our relationships are based on more than just a hard penis."

Like the preceding boyfriend, Tom from Chicago, Jeff was nearly ten years younger than Leonard. The couple dated steadily on a long-distance basis for almost two years. But once again, Leonard was the one to break things off. When Jeff said to him, "I love coming here to see you, but I don't know if I like you or the trees at the river better," Leonard immediately put up a wall. He was not going to allow himself to get hurt again, just in case Jeff decided in favor of the trees rather than him.

For several years things went well for Matlovich in Guerneville. But then a disease called AIDS invaded the gay community, and the Russian River was one of the many places hit hard by the epidemic. As more and more gay men came down with the disease, concern mounted, and as publicity in the local and national media increased, concern disintegrated into hysteria. Because so little was known about AIDS in those early years, this hysteria was not surprising. It was hardly justifiable, however, and Matlovich was but one of many who suffered for it.

"Every time the *Chronicle* or the *Examiner* featured AIDS horror stories, more people came to me and said that they really felt bad about it but they were afraid to eat in gay establishments. At first I tried to reason with them. I told them that I didn't think that they could catch anything in my place; it seemed to be a sexually-transmitted disease. But none of us knew for sure back in '83. We didn't have a lot of information

"Back in '81, soon after I left San Francisco and went to the river to open the restaurant, AIDS was a thing that I heard about occurring only in New York. I also remember feeling cocky, because I thought that the only people who needed to worry were those who went to the bathhouses or used drugs. Of course, history proved me wrong. Had I known, even a year later, what was to happen, I never would have gotten into the food business in the first place for fear of AIDS. I had too much to lose."

Scott Kersnar agreed that Matlovich had a great deal to lose:

"Other gay leaders thought Leonard was being hysterical about the impact of AIDS on the Russian River community, but I think he had justifiable concerns. He had a very visible place, after all. His Bronze Star was hanging on the wall as well as his framed copy of *Time* magazine, and his business suffered because of it. Both at his place and at other restaurants, people would call up and ask, 'Is your cook gay?' If the answer was yes, that was it. It definitely made things difficult for Leonard economically."

AIDS affected Leonard's business so severely that in early 1984 he sold the restaurant and returned to San Francisco. He didn't want to leave Guerneville, but he felt he had little other choice. He soon learned that San Francisco was hardly the place to escape the AIDS crisis.

9

A Time of Struggle

As soon as Matlovich returned to San Francisco, he became embroiled in the bathhouse issue. For years, gay men in San Francisco and elsewhere had patronized a wide variety of bathhouses and sex clubs, which had grown out of the heady, freewheeling lifestyle of the 1970s. According to journalist Randy Shilts, the baths were "convenience stores for quick cavorting" which comprised a $100 million industry spread across the United States and Canada. In San Francisco alone, patrons could choose between dozens of such establishments, including Bulldog Baths, which advertised itself as the largest bathhouse in the world; the independently-operated Club Baths at Eighth and Howard, which regularly served three thousand customers a week; and the branch of the Club Baths chain on Ritch Street, which could easily accomodate eight hundred pleasure-seekers at once.

For a long time the baths were accepted by most members of the gay community as a legitimate part of the social and sexual fabric. But with the arrival of AIDS, many began to view them with an increasingly critical eye. True, there was no known correlation between bathhouse attendance and AIDS, but many believed that the likelihood of high-risk sexual behavior was greater at the baths than elsewhere, and therefore that they should be shut down for the public good. At the very least, the owners should be forced to distribute educational materials and to post warnings about the disease.

Leaders of the Harvey Milk Democratic Club were the first to raise the issue publicly in March 1983, when Matlovich was still living in Guerneville. Their pleas for the distribution of safe sex materials and literature were angrily rejected by most bathhouse owners, however. Concerned about the upcoming annual Lesbian and Gay Freedom Day Parade in June, when hundreds of thousands of visitors would descend upon the city, the Milk Club leaders took their concerns to the gay press instead.

A letter sent by these leaders to the editor of the *Bay Area Reporter (B.A.R.)*, a gay newspaper, led to an uproar in the community. The rival Alice B. Toklas Democratic Club firmly opposed the Milk Club's efforts to "dictate" sexual mores to the community. The co-chair of the Freedom Day Parade, Konstantin Berlandt, decried what he considered to be a deliberate effort to turn back the progress of the sexual revolution. Eventually, even the mayor and the public health director got involved. But nothing was done about the baths until the following year, for no one agreed what should be done. In the meantime, bathhouse attendance declined, and two bathhouses shut down for lack of business.

Then in March 1984, a gay activist named Larry Littlejohn, a former president of the Society for Individual Rights and currently a deputy sheriff for the city, decided to do something about the issue. He launched a drive to prohibit sexual activity in the city's bathhouses by putting an initiative on the November ballot requiring the Board of Supervisors to adopt an ordinance to that effect. Leonard Matlovich was one of those he consulted. Recalls Matlovich:

"I knew from reading Randy Shilts' articles in the *Chronicle* how he felt about the bathhouse issue, and when I heard about Larry Littlejohn's efforts, I decided to help. I met with them both, and we planned strategy. Of course, none of us wanted to see the election actually take place. From my experience in Florida, I knew how dangerous it was to let the people vote on matters of civil rights, and the same thing held true for matters of public health. We just wanted to see the bathhouses closed down, and we knew that sometimes you need an impetus, a catalyst of some sort, to motivate people to do something. So we decided to force the mayor's hand. With the Democratic Convention coming to town that fall, the last thing she wanted was a referendum on the bathhouses in San Francisco.

"Unfortunately, not everyone wanted to see the bathhouses closed. Some people argued that they were a place to educate. But I thought it was a far better strategy to close the places down first and then to educate, because a lot of people wouldn't have paid attention otherwise. Furthermore, I thought it was very foolish for our community to start drawing battlelines at the bathhouses, for they were a difficult issue to defend. As soon as the AIDS crisis developed, I saw that this would be a magnificent political issue for the right-wing oppressors. They couldn't wait to drag our private sex lives into public view.

"Besides, I never understood the need for bathhouses in the first place. Before I came out of the closet publicly, I had never even heard of them. I didn't know they existed. To this day, I have only entered two bathhouses in my life, one in Kansas City and one in Miami, and all I did was look around. My guides were bath owners who were helping to fund the fights against Anita Bryant and John Briggs. Nevertheless, I never had any emotional feelings about the bathhouses one way or the other. In fact, one of my heroes in the gay movement is Jack Campbell of Miami, the man who founded the Club Baths chain. He has given selflessly to the movement without ever asking for anything in return. Everything he earned in the bathhouses he has repaid a hundred fold back to the community.

"But when I challenged the Air Force, I did it to establish certain rights for gay people — the right of employment, of housing, of public accommodations, and the like. I did not do it to promote public sex houses or commercialized sex. That has no meaning to me whatsoever in terms of liberation. My civil rights do not depend on the bathhouses being open any more than they depend on the moon rising in the west and setting in the east.

"You know, when I first moved to San Francisco, I was constantly accosted by people offering pot, crystal, and every type of drug imaginable right outside my front door whenever I walked up the street. At first I thought, 'How fabulous. How wonderful to live in a city so liberal that people are allowed to do what they want without interference from others.' But then I noticed that the same thing wasn't happening on Union Street, the straight equivalent to the Castro. Neither was it happening in other 'nicer' straight parts of town. Soon I began to realize that the reason the drug pushers were on Castro Street was not that people were so tolerant but that they just didn't care. In that case, I decided, what was happening was not liberation but oppression. When people ignore your health, it's not a sign of love but of indifference.

"It was the same thing with the baths. If the city officials truly cared about our health — if AIDS were a predominantly straight disease — the bathhouses would have been closed down a long time ago. They would have closed so fast our heads would have swum."

In an interview he gave to Shilts for the *Chronicle*, in which he was described as "one of the nation's best-known gay leaders" as well as a "gay hero," Matlovich reduced his argument to one basic truth, as he saw it. "If we don't save our own people from this terrible disease, nobody else will," he stated. "We have to clean up our act in our own community. People are dying and we have to start saving lives." He then announced his intention to collect signatures for the initiative on the street corner.

Despite this attempt to force her hand, the mayor refused to act, saying it was a matter for the Department of Public Health to decide. The following day, though, the director of that department, Merv Silverman, called the initiative a "political nightmare" and added that educational efforts within the gay community were the only effective means of stopping AIDS. Even the Milk Club leaders balked. Carol Migden, president of the club, called the measure "bothersome" and said, "I don't think it's appropriate to decide public health policy by ballot measures. . . . It's a sensitive issue about the state policing sexual behavior." And Cleve Jones, Harvey Milk's former lieutenant who by 1984 was serving as an aide to California Assemblyman Art Agnos, called the ballot proposal "legislating morality."

Horrified by the prospect of a public vote on the issue, gay leaders joined together to block the initiative, as Littlejohn, Matlovich, and Shilts hoped they would if city officials did nothing. Supervisor Harry Britt, Community College Board President Tim Wolfred, and officers of the San Francisco AIDS Foundation, Bay Area Physicians for Human Rights, the Pride Foundation, and the Harvey Milk and Alice B. Toklas Democratic Clubs all signed a statement asking the baths to close voluntarily. Although bathhouse owners did not accede to this request, on April 10, Merv Silverman announced that he had the community support he needed to do something about the baths. Flanked by over twenty leaders of the gay community, he stated his intention to draw up regulations banning sex in the bathhouses and private clubs.

Once again, passions were ignited, and the gay community was split by the controversial issue. Shilts was branded "the most homophobic press person in the Bay Area" by Toklas President Randy Stallings. Matlovich, on the other hand, was portrayed by the Sisters of Perpetual Indulgence, a satirical order of gay men dressing as nuns, as a fascist on placards that they paraded around the city. Another vehement opponent of the bathhouse reformers was Paul Lorch, the editor of the *Bay Area Reporter*, who issued the following inflammatory call to arms:

"The Gay Liberation Movement in San Francisco almost died last Friday morning at 11 a.m. No, that's not quite it. The Gay Liberation Movement here and then everywhere else was almost killed off by 16 Gay men and 1 Lesbian last Friday morning. ... This group would have empowered government forces to enter our private precincts and rule over and regulate our sex lives. ... The Gay Community should remember those names well — if not etch them into their anger and regret. ... These people would have given away our right to assemble, our right to do with our own bodies what we choose, the few gains we have made over the past 25 years. These 16 people would have killed the movement — glibly handing it all over to the forces that have beaten us down since time immemorial. ... The people of the community were quick to see what was being traded off, and have responded in anger and consternation. This office has received more mail on this issue than any other. Not one letter backed the collaborators."

In a subsequent issue of the *B.A.R.*, reporter George Mendenhall claimed that eleven of the gay leaders who originally backed Silverman later had reservations or misgivings about doing so. The *B.A.R.* also quoted a *San Francisco Examiner* survey, which indicated that thirty-four percent of the overall gay population favored measures to ban bathhouse sex, and only eighteen percent thought they should be closed. Faced with this kind of opposition, Silverman backed off once again. Several months later, however, in September, he ordered fourteen bathhouses closed for violating the regulations he had previously instituted. Then in October he invoked emergency powers to close the baths outright. The bathhouse owners sued. Superior Court judges intervened. For months, the issue was unresolved. Eventually, the community lost interest and most of the bathhouses closed for lack of customers. According to Pulitzer Prizewinning author Frances Fitzgerald, not only was this a result of changing sexual practices, but "the baths had lost their symbolic value" as "synecdoches for gay sexual freedom."

Leonard Matlovich was not in San Francisco to see the resolution of the conflict he helped to generate, however. In early 1984, soon after giving his interview to Shilts, he decided to visit an old Air Force buddy in Germany for a month. On the way, he stopped off in Florida to visit his parents, and when he returned, he planned to relocate permanently to Washington, D.C.

The move back East was triggered by an invitation from a group of fellow gay conservatives in Washington to help form a gay conservative organization which would lobby Congress on behalf of gay rights concerns. He had even been nominated as the probable figurehead of the organization. The name of the group was to be Concerned Americans for Individual Rights (CAIR), and backers of the idea included such prominent, if controversial, figures as Robert Bauman, a former congressman from Maryland who came out of the closet only when arrested for having sex with teenage hustlers, and Terry Dolan, the founder of the National Conservative Political Action Committee, who never did come out of the closet, even after he came down with AIDS in 1985.

For several months, Leonard delayed his trip to Europe while he discussed the technicalities of setting up CAIR. Unfortunately, he soon crossed swords with Bruce Decker, a gay Republican "bigwig" from California and one of Terry Dolan's close personal friends, over the bathhouse issue. When Decker read in the *Chronicle* that Matlovich was supporting Littlejohn's initiative, he used his influence to prevent Leonard from being offered the job as the head of CAIR. Matlovich tried to take a detached view of the situation.

"When I attended the first meeting of CAIR supporters, I thought, 'God, the power in this room is incredible.' There were a lot of influential people within the Reagan administration there, both Reagan's personal friends as well as his political appointees. But they were all so terribly closeted that it was hard to do anything. How do you form a gay political organization with a Board of Directors of twenty or thirty people when only two are willing to put their names on anything?

"It's not just a conservative thing, though. The two liberal gay congressmen from Massachusetts were also reluctant to admit their homosexuality until forced to do so. Gerry Studds was dragged out of the closet, and Barney Frank didn't come out until after Bob Bauman wrote about him in his book. Still, it's harder to be an openly gay Republican than it is to be an openly gay Democrat, because the Democrats have done their homework. And that's what CAIR was supposed to be about — educating and teaching people, trying to change their attitudes and behavior. Due to their closeted attitude, internal bickering, and other issues, however, CAIR never got off the ground."

Frustrated but resigned, Matlovich left Washington and flew to Germany to visit his friend in April 1984. Since he no longer had an immediate reason to return to the United States, when his Air Force buddy suggested that he find a job in Europe, Leonard took his advice. He took his discharge papers to the civilian personnel office of the U.S. Army base in Heidelberg and pestered them until they found him something to do. Since his discharge had been upgraded to honorable, and since he still had his Bronze Star and Purple Heart, he was well qualified for anything the Army could offer him. What they offered, however, surprised even him.

"The people at Civilian Personnel didn't recognize my name, not that I know of. I didn't lie or anything. I just filled out the papers. Then they gave me a job supervising high school kids in a summer hire program. When they told me I'd be supervising teenagers, mostly American teenagers, I literally almost passed out on the floor. But I'd had plenty of experience with kids in the Mormon Church, so I wasn't going to worry about it if they weren't.

"Most of the jobs the kids were assigned involved grounds-keeping on the army base, which was a lot of fun. Even better, the U.S. Army was paying me eight dollars an hour to live in Europe. When I wasn't working, therefore, I had enough money to travel on the weekends. My Air Force buddy, his lover and I would take off and go all over Europe — or as far as we could get in a weekend. That job lasted three months."

At the end of the summer, the teenagers he was supervising went back to school, but Leonard soon found another job, this time as a car salesman with the Ford Motor Company in Augsburg. He didn't speak German, but since he would be dealing mainly with American G.I.s, that didn't matter. He loved cars with a passion, and he looked foward to selling them.

Just as Leonard was about to start that job, however, Robert Bauman, the former congressman from Maryland who had worked with Matlovich to establish CAIR, arrived for a visit. Bauman told Matlovich that there was a chance of reinstituting CAIR and that once again he was being considered to head the organization. Leonard was reluctant to return to Washington, for he had grown to enjoy life in Europe, but he felt a responsibility to go back. He had taken part in the fight to preserve the gay rights ordinance in Miami and the struggle to defeat the Briggs Initiative in California, he reasoned; at a time when the gay community faced its biggest crisis ever — AIDS — he could not sit idly by in Europe enjoying himself. When he returned to Washington and attended his first CAIR meeting, however, the same people were trying to overcome the same difficulties they had failed to overcome when Matlovich left. So Leonard looked around for something else to do.

"That's when I did the same thing in Washington that Larry Littlejohn did here. I filed the paperwork with the city to close down the bathhouses. It needed to be done, I felt. Nowhere in Washington at that time did you ever see anything about AIDS posted. There was no educational information of any kind in any gay establishment, much less the baths. Washington was years behind San Francisco in that regard. So I did what I thought would motivate other people to do something constructive about AIDS. I even registered as a Democrat and joined the Gertrude Stein Democratic Club because it was necessary if I wanted to have any say at all.

"Unfortunately, I was still a political novice in many ways, despite my years in the movement. I did my best to follow the correct political process, yet the gay leadership there was unanimously negative toward me. Although I had felt like a member of the Washington community ever since I first moved there ten years earlier, they treated me like an outsider coming in. Frank Kameny, the first openly gay man I ever talked to, called me on the phone and said, 'We're going to run you out of town on a rail.'

"In response, I met with the leadership of the community and tried to explain what I was trying to do. I told them that by no means did I want the initiative to go to an election, but they didn't understand. I think they had well-meaning motives for opposing me — they were afraid to give up something they had worked very hard to obtain — but still, I think they were wrong. We just had different philosophies. We were fighting for the same thing but in different ways."

Frank Kameny remembers the period vividly in a statement that reveals much of the bitterness felt by Washington's gay political leaders at the time:

"Leonard made the mistake, politically speaking, of coming back to Washington, where he had not been deeply involved and where he was something of an outsider. He started a campaign at the beginning of the AIDS epidemic to have us close the baths. That's not the way we do things here in Washington. We have our own politics and we handle them well. We're very proud of the way we handle them and believe we do a lot better than any other city in the country, including San Francisco. So Leonard's effort was taken in rather bad stead, in general, by the organized political gay community here. He pulled back in due time, of course. He was unsuccessful in his attempts to close the baths. But it did create for a short period of time a great deal of ill feeling, which fortunately has now passed."

Another friend and former ally of Matlovich who disagreed with him on the bathhouse issue was Miami's Jack Campbell, the founder of the Club Baths chain. Admits Campbell:

"I was surprised he was taking that position. I'm not really sure why he did. I guess I didn't realize that Leonard is as politically conservative as he is. I didn't see him throughout that period, but when I finally did run into him again in a restaurant in Washington, I knew that he had been castigated rather severely in the gay press. I never even brought it up to him. It never came between us as friends."

According to Randy Shilts, one reason Matlovich failed to bring about the closure of the baths in Washington was that he failed to accurately assess the role the media had played in San Francisco:

"In San Francisco, the [Littlejohn] initiative resulted in the closing of the baths. One reason is that the day after the petition was taken out it was on the front page of the *Chronicle*, so everybody had to address the issue seriously. Public officials were forced to take sides. That's not what happened in Washington when Lenny tried to do the same thing there. In Washington, the *Post* didn't cover it. I think they buried it away with a couple of grafs. They were going to be nice liberal journalists who sneered at closing the bathhouses as a conservative thing to do. From my point of view, though, being liberal means you let gay businessmen murder gay people. By not covering the issue, the *Post* pulled out one of the key linchpins of Lenny's strategy. As a result, Lenny's efforts failed, and he was crucified in the local gay press by the typical knee-jerk gay activist response to his initiative."

For Matlovich, the animosity of Washington's gay community was difficult to take:

"I never felt so politically alone in my life as I did in Washington. The conservatives fired me from my job because they said the state has no right to stop people from doing what they want, and the liberals were angry for the same reasons. The *Washington Blade*, the gay newspaper there, did a real hatchet job on me. They said things that weren't true without even interviewing me. I thought I would get support from someone, but I got none at all, except for one gay dentist who wrote a very forceful letter to the *Blade* on my behalf. But that's all right, for I was proud of my stand. In no way did I regret it, for I think I did the right thing. Besides, as Harry Truman said, 'If you can't stand the heat, get out of the kitchen.'

"Nevertheless, the personal abuse I received did hurt. When the Sisters of Perpetual Indulgence crucified me for my stand on the baths, for instance, that hurt, because I'm genuinely committed to the gay rights cause, and I don't think it helps to attack each other all the time. The traitor list that the *B.A.R.* published was a particularly sad example of our divisiveness. Perhaps I come in for more than my fair share of abuse because I'm so conservative and outspoken. But other leaders get the abuse as well. It's part of being a public figure. In any case, there have obviously been more positive strokes than negative ones for me, or I wouldn't have continued to speak out over the years. If all the responses were negative, I just couldn't do it."

With the failure of CAIR and of the bathhouse intiative, Leonard saw no reason to remain in Washington any longer. In November of 1985, he returned to San Francisco, this time for good.

Fighting for His Life

Returning to his apartment at Eighteenth and Castro, Matlovich salvaged something from the frustrations of the previous year and a half. Using the connections he established with the Ford Motor Company in Augsburg, the company he would have worked for had he stayed in Europe, he landed a job selling cars for S&C Ford on Market Street. As usual, Leonard threw himself into his job with the same kind of energy and drive that he devoted to all his endeavors. The result was yet another award, this time as "Salesman of the Month."

For nearly a year he led a quiet life, selling cars during the day and meeting with friends or attending political meetings at night. He worked long hours, sometimes as many as fourteen hours a day, seven days a week, but he didn't mind. He had always enjoyed hard work. In fact, in spite of his long hours, he still had time and energy enough to devote to yet another project, this one a memorial to gay and lesbian Vietnam veterans.

Matlovich had been thinking about such a memorial for over ten years, ever since he lived in a house three blocks away from Congressional Cemetery in Washington, D.C. To relax in those days, he would wander through the cemetery looking for the graves of the famous people who were buried there. One day he ran into a person who was looking for the grave of Walt Whitman's lover, Peter Doyle. He was amazed and impressed that anyone would do that — not just look for the grave of a famous gay person but for the grave of that person's lover as well. He realized then that there were no permanent memorials, such as gravesite monuments or public statuary, for openly gay people in this country, and an idea was born. He decided to create his own memorial, not just for gay people in general but for gay veterans in particular.

The idea took further shape when the AIDS crisis spread and Leonard began to consider the possibility of his own death. He decided that the simplest way to fulfill his goal was to use his own future gravesite as the site of the memorial. In 1984, while living in Washington D.C., he bought a plot for himself in Congressional Cemetery for nine hundred dollars. He then planned the design of the memorial, which would double as his tombstone, and saved money for its execution. Two years later, in late 1986, the monument was completed and installed at a cost of three thousand dollars. Matlovich was more than pleased with the finished product.

The memorial is a simple slab of black granite inset with two pink granite triangles at the top. The triangle at the left, identical to the triangles which gay people were forced to wear in the concentration camps of Nazi Germany, points downward. In military symbolism, this is a sign of defeat. The triangle at the right points upward, a sign of victory. Beneath the two triangles are chiseled the phrases, "Never Again" and "Never Forget." Below the triangles, Leonard's birthdate appears.

There is no name on the tombstone — simply the words, "A Gay Vietnam Veteran." This is followed by a statement: "When I was in the military they gave me a medal for killing two men and a discharge for loving one." It was a quote that Matlovich used for years, at fundraisers, rallies, and political events. It was, he acknowledged, "a standard line." He explained further:

"When I placed the headstone, I had it done anonymously, because I wanted to honor those who served in Vietnam. I really didn't want to be seen as self-serving. Had I died in Vietnam when I hit the mine, I would have been just another dead Vietnam vet, you see. I would not have been a specifically *gay* Vietnam veteran who died for his country. I knew there were thousands of gay veterans like me who would be proud to be remembered not only for their sacrifice but also for their sense of self-worth as gay people. I wanted it to be their monument as well as my own.

"Even though many people recognized the quote and knew that the headstone must have been mine, I would not have acknowledged it for years if something had not happened to make me alter my plans. But something did happen almost immediately, so in early 1987 I went public with it. That's when I decided to add my name at the foot some day. My father wants me to add 'Mission Accomplished' as well. When he suggested that, I felt like a million dollars, because it showed how supportive he is of what I've done.

"When I bought the plot, I left room for two, because I still hope to have a lover some day. I would love to have two names on there so we could make love for all time. Heaven to me would be spending the rest of eternity traveling all over the universe and visiting all the wondrous spots with a lover at my side.

"As it is now, though, I'll have to be content with the company of J. Edgar Hoover and his boyfriend, Clyde Tolson. They aren't buried together, but J. Edgar is buried just down the row, and Clyde is buried right next door to me, which is as close as he could get to Hoover. I've already talked to Clyde about it in my dreams, and he says that when I move into the neighborhood, we can play footsies together, if nothing better comes along."

Shortly before placing the headstone, Matlovich learned that he might be "moving into the neighborhood" sooner than he thought, for he was diagnosed with AIDS in September 1986. At first he had thought it was simply a chest cold. He had no reason to think it was anything more serious, for he had none of the typical signs of AIDS — no swollen glands, fevers, night sweats, or unexplained weight loss. He *was* fatigued much of the time, but this he attributed to overwork and nothing more. Following a set of chest X-rays and a spume test, however, his doctor told him that he had pneumocystis carinii pneumonia, one of the diseases resulting from AIDS. This was the development that made him change his plans about acknowledging the headstone — that made him change his plans about everything. Suddenly, his entire world was altered, and he wasn't prepared to deal with it.

"I never worried about AIDS in the beginning, for I was sure it was associated with a lifestyle that I didn't share — bathhouses, drugs, that sort of thing. I never messed around very much; I might have had seven sex partners a year, and they were all people I was dating. True, when I first moved to San Francisco, you couldn't keep me out of the bars, but that doesn't mean I went home with anyone. I'm a perfect example of 'A little dab'll do ya.'

"Besides, none of my friends had it. The first person I knew who got AIDS was a former roommate at the Russian River. But that wasn't until 1986. As far as I know, I still don't have any close friends with AIDS, and I don't know of anyone I've been to bed with who has come down with it either. I was the first of my circle to get it."

As soon as Leonard was diagnosed, he was treated on an outpatient basis and advised to return to work, for his case of pneumocystis was a mild one. Unfortunately, he had an allergic reaction to the medicine he was given, and, a week after his diagnosis on September 15, he was admitted to the hospital. There he developed a yeast infection and lost forty pounds. Despite these setbacks, he was not frightened. He didn't even tell his parents he was sick, for he always believed he would pull through. His roommates, who were not so certain, told his mother for him. His father, who had been kept in the dark to spare his feelings, found out almost the exact same way he found out that Leonard was gay many years before — he saw the news on TV.

"Fortunately, my family reacted well and has been very supportive all along. They're sad, but positive. In fact, my having AIDS has brought us all closer together. The problem is that we've never communicated well in my family. Because I was gay, there was always a wall. I never did sit down and talk with my parents about why I am gay. I still haven't done that. After so many years of not talking about it, it's hard to start now.

"Once, my mother said, 'God, I wish we had known you were gay. We would have gotten you help a long time ago.' And I said, 'Thank God you didn't, for you wouldn't have gotten me the kind of help I needed. You would have gotten me a psychiatrist, and that would really have been terrible.'

"My parents won't even visit me in San Francisco. They hate it here and consider it the source of all my problems. I guess it's because they did come here once, and when they saw guys walking up and down Castro Street displaying their wares, they really weren't ready for it. I learned then that you have to be careful what you let your parents know about the gay scene, even though it's important to come out to them. Most can handle the fact that you are gay, but they can't always handle the details. My father once asked my mother what she thought I did in bed, for instance, and my mother said, 'Don't ask me. I don't know — and I don't want to know.'

"Having AIDS makes all this even more difficult, for families have to face up to certain things that were previously left undiscussed. In my case, it seems to be working out for the better. My diagnosis has not diminished the love my family has for me but has increased it. My friends have also reacted positively. I can honestly say that for me AIDS has not been a negative experience. Oh, there has been pain, sickness, hospitalization, and helplessness, but as far as having my clothes burned or people having nothing to do with me, it just hasn't happened."

After three weeks on the drug pentamidine, Leonard was well enough to return to work. He soon found that it was too tiring, however. On December 2, the same day he began taking the experimental drug AZT, he quit his job at S&C Motors. After that, he lived on disability and savings.

Looking around for something to do with his time, Matlovich began speaking out on AIDS issues and quickly became known as an AIDS activist. At first his message was a frightening one.

"In the beginning, I thought we had better arm ourselves, because there are forces out there that are using this as an excuse to do us in. I get a lot of right-wing literature in the mail, because I want to know exactly what the opposition is thinking about, and what they are thinking about is AIDS. But they're actually more interested in our lifestyle than they are about AIDS. It's our lifestyle they want to eliminate, not the disease. So they say that AIDS is a result of that lifestyle, that it's a punishment from God, and we deserve it. Using God's name allows them to feel self-righteous and justifies whatever they say or do, however evil.

"Although I've never fallen for the conspiracy theories about AIDS, I definitely fear the concentration camps. 'Health camps,' they would probably call them. After all, this country did lock up over 100,000 Japanese-Americans during World War II, and I think the religious right wing would be happy to put us away in similar camps in the name of God. This could very easily become a serious threat. The only way for evil to reign is for people of good will to say nothing. Well, I'm not going to be a good Jew and go to the gas chambers. No way."

While Matlovich's concentration camp fears were considered extreme by many in the gay community, he tempered this message of impending Apocalypse with a message of hope and faith, the same kind of upbeat propoganda he had been preaching for years, especially when the community faced a defeat or a setback.

"If there has to be a disease, and if I have to have it, then this is the disease I want, because the good that has come out of it is just incredible. The reality of the situation is that before we meet, the main thing gay people have in common is our sexuality. Yet the AIDS crisis allows us to share far more by bringing us closer together. For this much love, care, and compassion to come out of this community because of AIDS proves that we truly are a people of incredible love. We're going to be a better community because of this.

"Since I've had AIDS, I've seen so much to admire. We've developed so many support groups and buddy systems. People don't have to do these things, but they do. Not long ago, for example, I saw a gay couple on a talk show on TV. One had AIDS and the other didn't, and when the commentator expressed surprise that the healthy lover was staying with the one with AIDS, the healthy one said, 'Yes, I'm staying with him. You think I should leave him? I love him.' Since we have no family ties that keep us together — only love — it's incredible.

"Later, I ran into a doctor who works at a Southern Baptist hospital in Atlanta who said, 'I didn't think gay people were capable of so much love.' That's another of the positive aspects of AIDS — not just that we are expressing our love so freely for one another but that the straight community is perceiving us as people of love at last. AIDS will affect every family in this country eventually, and I think even they are beginning to realize that there are many things they can learn from us when it comes to dealing with this crisis."

While preaching gay love and pride to his listeners, Matlovich also reminded them that the health crisis is a political problem that calls for political action. Leonard hardly sounded like a loyal Republican when he said:

"The people in the Reagan administration certainly aren't doing anything to lead this nation through this crisis. When three young boys with AIDS in Florida were burned out of their home, Reagan didn't do anything about it. I don't think he even condemned it. Had the same thing happened to almost any other minority, the reaction would have been entirely different.

"You know, people talk a lot about the Iran-Contra Affair, but I think the Reagan administration will not be judged so much by that affair as by its lack of response to AIDS. When faced with Legionnaire's disease and toxic shock syndrome, the government moved so fast that people's heads swam. Well, it didn't happen with AIDS. Because the disease was perceived as a gay problem, the government denied it until it moved into the straight community, just like it denied the drug problem in America when it was perceived as a black problem and not a white one.

"My Democratic friends often make fun of me for sounding like them when I criticize so strongly the man who is the leader of my own political party. I reply that you can't condemn all Republicans for the policies of one man, even if that man is the president. Senator Lowell Weicker, for instance, is one of our greatest allies in the fight against AIDS. And what about the many Democratic politicians who drag their feet on the AIDS issue? Naturally, I wish that Reagan, a man I once admired, had set a better example for others to follow, but as it is, I'm not going to waste any time crying over spilt milk. Instead, I'm going to get there and do something about what I consider to be a criminal situation."

Feeling this way, Matlovich decided to do more than just speak. In June 1987, he took to the streets in an effort to practice what he preached. This time he was not content to "rally the troops" in hotel lobbies, as he had done in the 1970s, or to march down Market Street to San Francisco's City Hall. Instead, he flew to Washington to confront Reagan directly by protesting in front of the White House. The method he chose was nonviolent civil disobedience. It was a radical move for the former airman-turned-activist, but times had changed drastically. He was no longer simply demanding his rights; he was fighting for his life.

Matlovich flew to Washington at the suggestion of Paul Boneberg, a San Francisco gay activist who was helping to organize the protest against the Reagan administration's AIDS policies. The protest was timed to coincide with the Third International Conference on AIDS at the Washington Hilton, which was attended by more than six thousand researchers, as well as by speakers such as Vice President George Bush. Converging on the capital were activists from across the nation, including Leonard's old friend, Troy Perry of the Metropolitan Community Church. The group was led by Dan Bradley, the head of the Legal Services Corporation during the Carter administration.

After marching from a downtown church to Lafayette Park, the 350 protestors participated in what the *Washington Post* called "an emotional rally" in front of the White House. There they demanded more funding and education for AIDS. Then they attempted to block traffic by sitting in the middle of Pennsylvania Avenue. Sixty-four demonstrators were promptly arrested by police wearing yellow rubber gloves to guard against infection. Matlovich was one of those arrested. The next day, he appeared on the front page of the *Post*, wearing an Air Force jacket decorated with medals and carrying an American flag as he was handcuffed by a policeman in riot gear. In the accompanying article he was quoted, "If I can spend three years fighting for democracy in Vietnam, I can spend an hour in jail fighting for our lives."

Actually, he spent no time in jail. Charged with disorderly conduct, he was released several hours later after paying a fifty dollar fine. Still, he had crossed a very important line.

"I had never been arrested before. It was quite an experience. One thing I learned that the other protestors and the police learned a long time ago was that it's basically a show. It's choreographed. First you negotiate with the Police Department. You promise to do your part and they'll do theirs. You get the free publicity, and they get the extra money. But it works. We were well covered in the media, as well we should have been, for this was the first time that people with AIDS ever did such a thing.

"For a conservative Republican who has always believed in law and order, it was an incredible experience to break the law deliberately. But I would do it again and again, for I was always too much of a goody two-shoes before. This doesn't mean that I'm a radical now. I don't want to tear the system apart. I still love this country with all my heart and soul, for it's been extraordinarily good to me. But it could be better, and I guess I've finally come to realize that while you can work through the system sometimes, there are other times when you have to buck the system. In my own way, I've been bucking the system for a long time. But I have a lot of pride in that, for it means that I've always been true to my convictions.

"If I am remembered for anything, I hope I am remembered for that. I believe it's very important to stand up and be counted. From our sacrifice we shall be known. If we are a community that's not willing to sacrifice, society will not change. Today's generation of gays and lesbians must make those sacrifices — we must go to jail if necessary — so that tomorrow's generations won't have to do that. How will history judge us if it sees that blacks were willing to be billy-clubbed, firehosed, and bitten by dogs, but that we didn't have the same commitment to our liberation?

"Fortunately, in Washington I saw that not only are we

making those sacrifices, but so is the next generation. When I agreed to participate in the demonstration, I thought I would know everyone who was going to get arrested, because I've been in the movement for twelve years. But I didn't know half the people there, for half were young people in their twenties. I thought this was fabulous, because it proved that people were not going back into the closet because of AIDS. They are meeting the challenge. It's wonderful to realize that although people like myself will no longer be a part of the picture some day, others will come into the movement to carry it foward."

Troy Perry, although equally as enthusiastic about the demonstration as Leonard, had a slightly different reaction:

"I went to Washington because of Leonard. I had seen him in San Francisco, and he told me about what was happening there. It was the first time I had seen him since his diagnosis, and he was in such good spirits. It was wonderful to see. But then, as I stood in Lafayette Park with my lover listening to Dan Bradley speak, the tears started. I just couldn't help it. There was Dan, and there was Leonard, two people I've worked with on gay rights issues over the years, and both of them had AIDS. I told my lover, 'I can't stand this, seeing my friends around me dying.'"

Perry was right to be concerned. From December 1986 to June 1987, Leonard's condition improved drastically, a change he attributed to AZT. Although he lost his endurance and found that he could easily sleep fourteen hours a day if he wanted, he kept as active as possible. But shortly after returning to San Francisco from Washington, he suffered a gall bladder attack on his birthday, July 6. He was rushed to the hospital, where he survived the attack but developed pneumonia and almost died. After three weeks, he was well enough to return home — at least until the next episode.

In the meantime, Matlovich made plans to attend the National March for Gay and Lesbian Rights to be held in Washington in October 1987. He ran into difficulties almost immediately, however, when he attempted to book a seat on Northwest Orient Airlines, the nation's fifth-largest airline. This was the airline that garnered international press attention in June when it refused to fly a person with AIDS from China to his home in Columbus, Ohio. The man was stranded in China until he was taken home on a United States Air Force plane — which cost his family forty thousand dollars. He died a week later. Matlovich knew none of this when he attempted to make his reservations, however.

"I was sitting at the house when a friend of mine came by. While he was here, I called up Northwest to make reservations to fly to the March on Washington, and he said, 'Don't you know they won't sell you a ticket because you have AIDS?' I thought he was kidding, but to keep him happy I asked the ticket agent on the phone if it was true. The agent said, 'That's correct.' I was literally speechless.

"I hung up the phone, but then I called back, for I knew this couldn't be right. I asked another agent the same question, and the second agent said, 'It's true. We can't sell you a ticket.' Then I got angry. So I called all the radio and television stations and the newspapers and said, 'Tomorrow at ten o'clock I'm going to be at the counter at Northwest Airlines trying to buy a ticket in person.' They still refused to sell me a ticket, even with the press there. So when I left the airport, I came right back and got a lawyer from Gay Rights Advocates and threatened to sue."

The reaction of Northwest officials was simple. They quoted an employee memo dated August 5 which said the airline would not "transport a passenger who is known to have a contagious disease." However, when Ken McPherson, a member of Mobilization Against AIDS, followed Matlovich's lead and requested a ticket after stating that he was gay and therefore "at risk" for AIDS, Northwest refused him a ticket as well but considered changing its policy. The year before, after all, Delta Airlines was the subject of a national boycott when they refused to fly a passenger with AIDS. That boycott ended only when Delta changed its policy and agreed to make financial contributions to AIDS organizations. Presumably, Northwest did not want to see the same thing happen to them.

A week after Matlovich's protest, therefore, Northwest hastily revised its policy. The new policy stated that the airline would fly people with AIDS, but only if such passengers provided a doctor's statement certifying that "the customer is medically fit to undertake the journey and does not pose a health risk to other passengers."

This was not enough for Leonard, who considered the new policy as blatantly discriminatory as the old one. It was also not enough for John Molinari of the San Francisco Board of Supervisors, who asked the city's district attorney to investigate the airline for violation of the city's anti-discrimination laws. Neither was it enough for the Human Rights Department of the state of Minnesota, which in September formally charged Northwest with illegally discriminating against people with AIDS. While Matlovich was appalled to see the airline steadfastly refuse to change its policy, he was pleased that others outside the gay community joined the fight to protect his rights.

"Some people said to me, 'Why did you have to tell them? They would never have known that you have AIDS.' I replied, 'So what about the person with visible lesions who can't hide his disease?' I just thought it was my moral obligation to tell them. It's like saying if there's a rule that Jews can't ride on airplanes, should Jews try to pass as Christians? I think that's immoral You have to fight. If we let this kind of thing happen without a challenge, even one time, things will only get worse. But if every time something like this happens there is a tremendous outcry of anger, a company will think twice before they establish a policy like this again.

"You know, it's a strange thing. When Northwest Orient Airlines refused to sell me a ticket, it was the first time in my entire life that I really felt discriminated against as a gay person. When I fought the Air Force, it didn't bother me as much, for I grew up in the military and knew what to expect. But with Northwest, I didn't expect it. I felt helpless. I don't ever want to feel that way again."

Anything but helpless, Leonard continued to speak out whenever the opportunity arose. In September, he took part in a demonstration against Pope John Paul II, who was visiting San Francisco as part of a highly-publicized tour of the United States. For months prior to this visit, the gay community was split by divided loyalties. Many were enraged not only by the pope's attitude toward homosexuality but also by his proposed — but eventually cancelled — visit to an AIDS hospice in the heart of the Castro, which they dismissed as nothing more than a publicity stunt devised to increase the pope's popularity. They also resented the public tax money being spent on his behalf. Others were equally passionate in their defense of the pope.

On the afternoon of September 17, San Franciscans had an opportunity to choose sides in the debate when the pope spoke to an audience comprised largely of specially-invited people with AIDS inside the basilica of Mission Dolores, the old Spanish church on the borders of the Castro. Outside, along Dolores Street, the pope's admirers were allowed to congregate. Nearby, on a single block of Sixteenth Street roped off by police barricades and patrolled by the Secret Service, the pope's opponents were allowed to gather and to speak. Leonard Matlovich was one of these.

"I spoke at the demonstration against the pope because I truly think that for a man who professes love, a lot of hatred drips from his lips, especially when it comes to our kind of love. John Wahl, the man who organized the demonstration, asked me to speak, and I considered it an honor. I will go anywhere anytime to speak against hypocrisy.

"Being an ex-Catholic had a lot to do with why I chose to speak. I was striking back for all those years of self-hatred that the church implanted in me. For years they lied to me, and they continue to lie today by telling people that what we do is a sin. So I stood up in front of that church and said, 'I am a good and moral person. I have a right to be here. You're the reason that gay people have for centuries been forced to meet in society's back alleys, because you denied us the right to stand up and affirm our feelings. You refused to validate our loving, caring relationships. No longer are we willing to accept this.'

"One thing that truly galls me about that pope is that he is one of those people, like Jerry Falwell, who says, 'Love the sinner, but hate the sin.' That kind of reasoning is merely an excuse to cover the real message, which is one of oppression. Neither the pope nor Jerry Falwell really cares about us. When the pope picked up that little boy with AIDS inside the Mission and newspaper editors across the country fell over themselves rushing to print it, do you think he really cared about that boy? No, it was great P.R., that's all. If he truly cared about people with AIDS, why didn't he hug some gay man as well? A lot of gay people were moved by the pope that day when he spoke of God's mercy and compassion. But I thought he showed more compassion toward Kurt Waldheim, a former Nazi, than he did to us.

"Still, we learned a lot that day, not only about the pope but also about effective public relations. For instance, one of the AIDS activists who attended the services in the Mission, Dan Turner, planned to hand the pope a condom when the pope shook his hand, in order to make a point. When I heard about it, I desperately tried to talk him out of it. On national TV, that would have come across terribly. You don't give the pope condoms. That would have turned off so many Catholics we would never have been able to recover. Fortunately, Dan changed his mind.

"I only wish the Sisters of Perpetual Indulgence had done the same about the satirical mass they held in Union Square earlier in the day. Like a lot of people, I think the Sisters are great comedy but terrible politics. They do us far more harm than good, because the homophobes accept them as the movement's chief spokespeople. Society will never take us seriously as long as this state of affairs continues. It's time for the leadership in this community to stand up against that. Of course, I would do nothing to stop them, and no one else should either, for they have a right to do what they want. But we have an equal right to disown them.

"Similarly, when we first heard about the pope's visit, a lot of people felt he didn't have the right to come here or to speak, but I totally disagreed, for I believe so strongly in freedom of speech. Yes, I was angry, but then I realized that the pope coming to the U.S. was one of the best things that ever happened to us. Because he came, we talked about all kinds of things that might never have gotten such wide public attention — gay and lesbian rights, women's issues, abortion, birth control, the nature of the priesthood, and related issues. He gave us an incredible forum and allowed us to educate thousands of people. As I said to friends, 'This is fabulous. He should come more often.'"

A few weeks after the pope left San Francisco, Leonard left too, this time for the March on Washington for Gay and Lesbian Rights in October. For most of the half million people who attended the weeklong series of events, the highlight was the march itself, which took place on October 11. For Matlovich, however, the highlight was a project which he initiated and organized, the Never Forget Project. Like the project he initiated to honor gay Vietnam veterans, once again Leonard was concerned with the creation of memorials for gay people. This time the focus was his former political antagonist, Harvey Milk.

"I was talking to Harvey's lover, Scott Smith, one day and found out that there isn't any memorial to him outside of San Francisco. In San Francisco, a library, a community center, and a public plaza are all named for him. But even here, there is no one particular spot that people go to pay their respects to Harvey Milk. I thought that was a shame, for people need to have a place to pay homage to a person they feel has made their lives better.

"Later, when news of my own tombstone hit the press, a friend suggested that I might do the same thing for Harvey that I did for gay Vietnam vets like myself — create a permanent memorial in a public cemetery. The idea for Never Forget evolved from that. But what really gave me the commitment to go through with it was remembering my visit to the cemetery where Alice B. Toklas and Gertrude Stein are buried in France. I was incredibly moved that Toklas and Stein, who were lovers, put their names on the same tombstone. I realized again that in this country we have nothing similar, and I determined to do something about it.

"I established Never Forget in order to create a kind of gay Arlington Cemetery, a place to bury and honor our heroes. And I chose Harvey Milk as the first of our leaders to honor because he did so much to inspire and motivate others. He was the movement's first true martyr. Even though Harvey never lived in Washington, Congressional Cemetery seemed like a logical place for the memorial because he was one of the first openly gay officials in the nation, and Congressional Cemetery is a place for national leaders. Besides, we'll never know, but had he lived, Harvey Milk might very well have been elected to Congress. In any case, when people visit San Francisco, they don't do so with the idea of honoring the dead. Yet in Washington, it's part of the psyche to visit national cemeteries.

"Because Harvey's ashes were scattered on the Pacific Ocean outside the Golden Gate Bridge after he died, there was no permanent gravesite anywhere, so we felt free to buy a plot for him in Washington. His lover, Scott Smith, had saved some of the ashes, so we placed those in an urn for Harvey, along with part of his ponytail, a love letter from him to Scott, a piece of his official stationery from City Hall, a copy of one of his speeches, and a photographic negative of him. On Saturday morning, the day before the march, we held a ceremony which was incredibly moving for me. Hundreds of people gathered to honor Harvey and to hear Troy Perry, Frank Kameny, Harry Britt, Morris Kight, and myself speak. Then we all filed by the gravesite and laid flowers in front of the urn itself. Many people cried openly.

"I suppose it is somewhat ironic that I was the one who organized the ceremony for Harvey, since we had our very major differences. However, like I said before, had Harvey Milk lived, I think he and I would have become friends. Besides, perhaps it was fitting for him to be honored by someone he once regarded as a rival. For Nixon to go to China made the gesture more valid than for a liberal Democrat to have gone. Maybe having a conservative person see the importance of what Harvey represented makes the memorial more significant.

"Now I hope other gay leaders will choose to be buried in Congressional Cemetery as well. I'm excited about it becoming our Arlington. Think what it will be like a hundred years from now for the young kid from Altoona, Pennsylvania, who Harvey always used to talk about, to visit the graves of his gay role models. Troy Perry has already talked with me about establishing a similar cemetery for the Metropolitan Community Church in Los Angeles. That way, we could have one on both coasts."

While in Washington, Matlovich also helped to lay wreaths

at the Tomb of the Unknown Soldier during a ceremony led by gay and lesbian veterans the morning of the march. There were no speeches for that event, which was simple and austere. For it, Leonard decided not to wear his Air Force uniform but his jacket from the Alexander Hamilton Post of the American Legion instead. The Alexander Hamilton Post, he proudly explained to anyone who asked, is the specifically gay branch of the American Legion which was established to prove not only that "We [gay people] Are Everywhere" but also that gay people can wave the flag as well as anyone. By joining this group, Matlovich was letting the world know that despite court battles, demonstrations, and arrests, he was at heart still a patriot, a true believer in what he called "the American way of life."

At the heart of the American way of life is the electoral process, and soon after Matlovich returned to San Francisco, he threw himself into the electoral fray for the second time. In November, following Art Agnos's election as mayor of San Francisco, Matlovich announced his "probable" candidacy for the state assembly seat vacated by Agnos. Although he had vowed never to run for office again following his decisive defeat in the 1980 supervisors' race, like many incipient and actual politicians he changed his mind a few years later.

"Brian Mavrageorge, the president of Concerned Republicans for Individual Rights, told me that a lot of people were pushing for me to run, because we needed to put up a gay Republican candidate to oppose the liberal Democrats who control this town. We wanted to show that people have a choice; just because they are gay doesn't mean they automatically have to vote Democratic. Other people told me they had never expected to vote Republican, but if I ran, they were going to vote for me. I was shocked at the amount of support I received. My candidacy would have drawn a lot of people into the Republican party.

"I also had my own personal reasons for running. I wanted to show that people with AIDS can still be productive human beings. We can still work and make society a better place. AIDS definitely would have been an issue, because a lot of people were concerned that I might not be able to carry out my duties. But one thing they needn't have worried about: after the election, I certainly wasn't going anywhere. With a shortened lifespan, I wasn't going to use the office to run for Congress the next time.

"In the long run, I decided not to enter the race. Because we are trying to build a real Republican party in San Francisco, we all decided to rally behind one candidate, and we chose Brian Mavrageorge instead. I was both disappointed and relieved not to be running. I knew I would miss the excitement of the campaign and the opportunity to serve, but at the same time I was glad that by not running I wouldn't have to watch what I said all the time. Since I wouldn't have a constituency to please, I could remain true to my convictions and wouldn't have to compromise. If a person like Martin Luther King had run for the Senate, for instance, he would have lost much of his ability to talk about the issues, because a lot of time when you tell the truth, people don't want to hear it."

After withdrawing from the campaign, Matlovich continued to speak "the truth" as he saw it. In January 1988, he was arrested for the second time in his life when he took part in a demonstration in support of the AIDS/ARC Vigil in San Francisco. For over two years, a group of people with AIDS and ARC had camped out on a patch of lawn in front of the old Federal Office Building on United Nations Plaza. Refusing to leave until certain demands were met (including more federal money for AIDS research and greater benefits for people with AIDS and ARC), the vigilers received enormous support, not only from the gay community but from the majority of San Francsico's elected officials as well. The federal government, however, did not acceed to their demands, and in December 1987 the vigilers, frustrated with government inaction, stepped up the level of protest by chaining themselves to the office building door, as they had done in the very beginning. In response, the government abandoned its two-year-old hands-off policy and arrested the protesters. Community leaders were quick to rally to their side.

Supervisor Harry Britt and Howard Wallace of the Gay and Lesbian Labor Alliance were two of the first gay leaders to be arrested on January 19. Matlovich was part of the second wave of "celebrity" protestors. Calling the vigilers "heroes," he was arrested on January 26 along with San Francisco Supervisor Nancy Walker; Pat Norman, the national co-chair of the March on Washington; Reverend Jim Sandmire of the Metropolitan Community Church; and Ben Schatz, an attorney for the National Gay Rights Advocates. Once again Leonard spent no time in jail. After being booked and ordered to pay a twenty-five dollar fine, he was set free. Unfortunately, coverage of the event in the local press was overshadowed by the demonstration and arrests at the nearby Burlingame offices of Burroughs-Wellcome, the makers of AZT, just a few days before. Nevertheless, Matlovich was proud to be a part of the growing national trend toward civil disobedience. It was true he was being radicalized, he told a friend, "but in a conservative sort of way."

For most gay San Franciscans, a Leonard Matlovich who was voluntarily arrested at an AIDS/ARC vigil was a great deal more palatable than one who represented conservative Republican interests. Consequently, the frequent antagonism he encountered in his early years in the city faded, and once again Matlovich began receiving awards from groups such as Federal Lesbians and Gays (FLAG). The reasons for this change of heart were obscure. Perhaps the community, mellowing in recent years, was not quite so eager to chew its leaders up and spit them out as it once had been. Perhaps, as Matlovich himself suggested, the gay community was much more diversified than other people believed, and there was always silent support for his point of view. Or perhaps it was simply easier for the community to view a person with AIDS sympathetically, no matter what his or her political stripe.

Whatever the reason, when Matlovich walked down Castro Street in 1988, he was much less likely than he had been a few years earlier to be accosted by a passing stranger hollering, "Who the fuck appointed you spokesperson for the community?" He was more likely to greeted by a friendly nod and a smile. Many were simply grateful that Leonard always had the courage to stand up for what he believed. Others were appreciative for a more specific reason.

"It's amazing how many people I've met and re-met over the

past twelve years who were playing a straight role the first time and who have come out of the closet since then. When they tell me, 'You had a lot to do with that,' it makes it all worthwhile. It's very satisfying to know that because I did something, people aren't suffering what I suffered. Maybe by helping them I've helped to make the world a better place."

Although he never realized what direction his idealism would carry him, "making the world a better place" was always one of Leonard's goals, ever since he joined the Air Force as a naive nineteen-year-old in 1963. Then, he thought he might someday fulfill his goal by making the world safe for democracy and the American way of life. Twenty-five years later he believed he had already fulfilled his goal by helping other gay people find pride and self-acceptance. But for an activist like Matlovich, no job is ever complete. There is always something to be done — and in 1988 that job was to continue to work to solve the AIDS crisis.

"I will go anywhere to discuss the issue. I'll do whatever I am asked to do. Primarily, I'd like to give hope to others, who, like myself, have the disease. Unlike others, I think hope is possible, for I do not view AIDS as a necessarily fatal disease. At first I did, but not any more. When I hear on TV that AIDS is fatal, I chuckle, for I know people — Dan Turner, for instance — who have been living for five or six years with AIDS. So we can battle it. Not only does their example justify my attitude, but so does the medical research that is being done, as well as my own experience with AZT.

"I certainly don't envision my own future as limited. There are so many things I'd still like to accomplish. I'd like to work in Washington D.C. for the government in an appointed position. I'd love to be involved in the Department of Defense, but I'd be happy to be in Health and Human Services or anywhere in the AIDS network so that I could help create policy and educate people. I'd also like a home with a yard, a picket fence, a dog, and perhaps some cats — somewhere around here preferably. And I wouldn't mind winning the California lottery. Above all, however, I'd like to have a lover. That, to me, would be heaven. I just want that feeling once in my life — to love and be loved wholeheartedly. I've never been involved with anyone long enough before to get past infatuation to love. If I had to, I'd move to Tupelo, Mississippi to experience it.

"In the meantime, I will continue to fight the epidemic to the best of my ability and to further the struggle for equal rights for gay and lesbian people. At times it's going to get rough, but I'm sure we're going to come out on top in the end, mainly because we're not going to go back into the closet no matter what happens. Society will soon be sophisticated enough to accept that. They will realize that they've either got to lock us up or set us free, and I don't think even this society would want to lock us all up. Actually, I think the future is going to be wonderful. I envy gay teenagers today, because I think they're going to have a much better world than we did. If some small part of that is due to the people who went before, so much the better. We did our part. With luck, the world will remember that we were around."

At the end of April 1988, no longer able to manage the climb to his third-floor flat in San Francisco, Leonard moved to West Hollywood to be with a friend who had promised to take care of him. After months of relative stability, Leonard's health was declining rapidly. AIDS was taking its toll. Leonard lost weight steadily, coughed frequently, and watched helplessly as K.S. lesions spread across his body. His illness affected his spirit as well as his body. According to his friend Michael Bedwell:

"A few months before he moved, Leonard gave up. I don't know if the physical deterioration was stimulating the sense of despair or vice versa, but whatever the reason, there was less joy and laughter in him. There were fewer new projects and ideas. He seemed to wind down.

"I was very surprised and concerned about his moving to L.A. at the end, but it was the kind of impulsive thing he did over and over again. Before he left, he gave me a remarkable number of things — things I think he would not have given up if he thought that death was a long way off.

"He still went through the motions, though. Two weeks after he moved, he returned to San Francisco for a fundraiser on Proposition 102. He also went to the March on Sacramento for Gay and Lesbian Rights in early May. His appearance there was really sad, for there was a pleading sound in his voice when he spoke to the crowd, as if this was his last chance to convey his message. His speech was a simple one. He said, 'We've got to love each other.' That's all.

"Shortly after that, he couldn't keep any food down. Besides fatigue, thrush, and K.S., his main problem was chronic diarrhea. He got so dehydrated that his friend Joe Ferrari, with whom he was staying, finally insisted that he go to the hospital. He was there for about a week. During that stay, his doctors discovered that the K.S. had spread internally. They gave him about three weeks to live.

"After Leonard returned home, Joe hired an attendant to stay with him during the day, even though he could still get around. When I visited soon after that, he was having a number of problems. He was beginning to show evidence of brain damage. Occasionally he was incoherent, and eventually he became nonconversant. He refused to speak on the phone or to see anyone if he could help it. He also resisted wearing clothes, and he stopped shaving or brushing his teeth, which wasn't like Leonard at all.

"The last couple of days he barely got out of bed. He began to experience cramps in his stomach, he developed bedsores, and he became incontinent. He refused all medicine, I think because he was afraid it would keep him alive longer. He knew he was going to die, and he didn't want to prolong it. He got weaker and weaker until he sunk into a kind of vegetative state. Finally, after several episodes of suspended breathing, he stopped altogether on Wednesday night, June 22, at 9:43 P.M."

Michael Bedwell, who was named executor of the estate, and Leonard's roommate, Joe, were only two of the people with Leonard when he died. Also present were Leonard's parents and a cousin. Other members of the family, his sister and two nieces, had visited shortly before his death. The cause of death was released by the family to the newspapers as "AIDS-related illnesses." Leonard was forty-four years old.

Eulogies immediately began pouring in from friends and admirers across the country. Ken McPherson, the friend who worked with him during the Northwest Airlines controversy, told the *San Francisco Examiner*, "[Matlovich's challenge to the

Air Force] transformed an entire generation. . . . Leonard stood for integrity. 'If you're an honorable person,' he said, 'then be yourself, don't be ashamed.'"

Bedwell added, "Leonard would want to be remembered for his struggles for peoples' civil rights, which grew out of his love for his country and his belief that the rights he had been taught to believe in applied to everyone." Concluded Lee Jenney, a friend from Washington and an official with Congressional Cemetery, "He was the most patriotic American I ever met. He had courage, strength, love, and compassion."

At Matlovich's request, his funeral was held in Washington D.C. on the Fourth of July, following an Episcopal mass at Christ Church. At the church, the Rev. Robert Nugent, a Roman Catholic priest, compared Matlovich to "political saints" such as Robert Kennedy, Martin Luther King, and Harvey Milk. The D.C. Gay Men's Chorus sang, and Charles Gibson, co-host of the ABC television program, "Good Morning America," spoke. Two hundred and fifty people attended.

Following the services, Matlovich was buried in nearby Congressional Cemetery with military honors. Despite his battle with the Air Force, as a veteran with an honorable discharge Leonard was entitled to a military funeral. Friends agreed that he would have been pleased with the results. As Frank Kameny told the *Washington Blade*, "The Air Force finally did it right and on Leonard's terms today. It's a pity that they didn't do it thirteen years ago."

The ceremony was a moving one. According to the *Blade*, a horse-drawn caisson carried Leonard's body to the cemetery. An eight-member honor guard served as pallbearers. Six Air Force riflemen fired three volleys in salute. Then an Air Force bugler played taps before a member of the honor guard presented the flag that draped Leonard's casket to his mother.

The gay presence at the funeral was just as significant as the military presence. Seven gay activists served as honorary pallbearers. Mourners carried lavender and rainbow-striped flags, symbols of the gay movement. Finally, a series of gay speakers addressed those gathered at the gravesite.

Among those speakers were Perry Watkins, Frank Kameny,

and Ellen Nesbitt, a lesbian fighting her own military discharge. Watkins, referring to Leonard's wartime tours of duty, said that foreign enemies in war were never as "bigoted and hateful" toward Matlovich as were his "homophobic" opponents in the United States. Kameny focused on the positive aspects of Leonard's career instead and said that he "greatly advanced" the gay rights cause. Nesbitt then urged the crowd to continue Matlovich's struggle for gay rights and to support the work he did as an AIDS activist. She also thanked Matlovich's parents "for instilling in Leonard so much love, courage, and self-respect."

At the conclusion of the service, Leonard's friends and relatives departed, leaving flowers and flags behind. Newspaper reporters made a few final notes while cemetery workers filled in the grave. Under the black granite headstone highlighted by two pink triangles, the man who was given "a medal for killing two men and a discharge for loving one" was at last laid to rest.

Subsequent Court Cases

Matlovich's challenge to the Air Force in 1975 was the first time a gay serviceman stood up and willingly acknowledged, "I am a homosexual," but it was not the last. Since then, hundreds of gay men and lesbians in the military have demanded the right to continue to serve in the armed forces without having to deny or to hide their sexual preference. The military, however, has remained adamantly opposed to their continued association. Since Matlovich first raised the issue, the military has not only fought those who have challenged its anti-homosexual policy in court; it has also gone out of its way to identify and oust suspected homosexuals in periodic witch hunts.

In the office files of the National Gay Rights Advocates in San Francisco, hundreds of newspaper clippings bear witness to this ongoing struggle. One after the other, the headlines proclaim, "Army Cans Gay 'Hero;'" "Airman Loses Appeal, Leaves Service;" "Army Fights To Keep Lesbian Out;" "Pentagon Issues New Ban on Gays;" and "U.S. Military Renews Witch Hunt for Gays." Only rarely does a headline read, "Lesbian Soldier Wins Court Case."

According to Matlovich's lawyer, David Addlestone:

"Except for the most recent case, all the cases since

Leonard's have been disasters. I've kept up with all of them, and it has distressed me to see one after the other go down. Unfortunately, I don't think the military will change their policy concerning gay people in the foreseeable future. They're so conservative now. For a while, during the Vietnam War, there was a warming period. Because the war was a bad experience for the military, the brass was thereafter sort of liberal in the way it dealt with the troops. But the services have gone back to the way they used to be — very macho and heterosexual. Homophobia is on the rise again. Rather than just issue discharges, they are court-martialing more and more people for homosexual acts.

"When Leonard issued his challenge, the Air Force wasn't going out of its way to prosecute gay people. At the time, we argued, 'If you're so damned concerned about it, why don't you really screen people? Why don't you go out and catch them all?' One of the themes of the case was hypocrisy. They didn't really care as long as you stayed in the closet and didn't tell them. We knew that many commanders just looked aside. When they had competent gay people working for them, they didn't give a damn. But that changed after Leonard's case. Perhaps Leonard's case set some of that off. Now they actually put gay bars off limits. They're more rigid. In today's military, a commander is much less likely to turn his head, because he may get caught and be blamed too."

A report released by the General Accounting Office (GAO) in October 1984 confirmed Addlestone's opinion that homophobia is on the rise in the military. From 1974 through 1983, 14,311 people were discharged from the military for being gay or lesbian. The first year of the survey, 1974, only 875 were discharged, but for the last four years covered by the report, nearly 2,000 a year were discharged. According to a more recent Pentagon study, 4,658 gay men and lesbians were discharged from 1985 through 1987. Almost half of these were from the Navy.

Other statistics in the GAO report substantiated Addlestone's remarks about the increasing aggressiveness of military persecution of gay people. From 1974 through 1978, for instance, investigations outnumbered discharges, but from 1979 through 1983 the opposite was the case, indicating that more and more discharges were the result of single, large-scale investigations. Partly due to the number of discharges, the average time of duty for gay men and lesbians in the services was less than that for straight servicemen and -women. During the time period covered by the GAO, homosexuals served for an average of only three years, while heterosexuals served for over five.

Recent developments verify that the military continues to purge gay people from its ranks. In late 1987, according to the *Advocate*, Air Force undercover agents invaded private homes and gay bars in the Netherlands to spy on suspected gay and lesbian personnel. This led the Dutch Parliament to demand an apology from the U.S. government, not only because in Holland homosexuality is legal, but also because Air Force officials were using the services of Dutch police to aid the investigations. And according to the *National Journal*, at approximately the same time, three female marines at the Parris Island recruit depot in South Carolina were suspended for homosexuality. Ten more were reported to be under suspicion. This is not uncommon, the magazine noted. In 1983, fifty-six enlisted men were interviewed at Bolling Air Force Base near Washington for homosexual activity. These are but a few of many similar examples.

Of course, the military makes no attempt to hide its opposition to gay servicemen and -women. And it is willing to pay dearly to keep them out. The $160,000 it paid Matlovich to settle his case was but a pittance compared to the millions of dollars it spends annually to train gay men and lesbians, only to oust them later. In 1983, the armed services spent $23 million to recruit and train the 1,796 homosexuals it later decided to expunge; another $370,000 was spent to secure their discharges.

While this opposition has remained resolute, for several years following the Matlovich challenge the military's specific policy regarding homosexuals waffled as the Department of Defense tried to come up with regulations that could withstand an increasing number of challenges from other gay men and lesbians in the service. In January 1981, the Department finally adopted the following regulations:

"Homosexuality is incompatible with military service. The presence in the military environment of persons who engage in homosexual conduct or who, by their statements, demonstrate a propensity to engage in homosexual conduct, seriously impairs the accomplishment of the military mission. The presence of such members adversely affects the ability of the military services to maintain discipline, good order, and morale; to foster mutual trust and confidence among service members; to insure the integrity of the system of rank and command; to facilitate assignment and worldwide deployment of service members who frequently must live and work under close conditions affording minimal privacy; to recruit and retain members of the military services; to maintain the public acceptability of military service; and to prevent breaches of security."

In most respects, this policy differs little from the Pentagon's traditional stance with regard to gay people. The main difference is that in 1981 the policy was broadened to include the clause concerning those "who, by their statements, demonstrate a propensity to engage in homosexual conduct." Before this clause was added, it was necessary for a service member to engage in homosexual conduct in order to be expelled. After 1981, simply professing homosexuality became grounds for expulsion.

Specifically, note the authors of the ACLU handbook, *The Rights of Gay People*, the 1981 regulations require the Department to discharge any service member who, "prior to or during military service, (1) 'engaged in, attempted to engage in, or solicited another to engage in a homosexual act'; (2) 'has stated that he or she is a homosexual or bisexual,' unless there is a finding that the individual is not a homosexual or bisexual; or (3) 'has married or attempted to marry a person known to be of the same biological sex,' unless there is a finding that the individual 'is not a homosexual or bisexual and that the purpose of the marriage attempt was the avoidance or termination of military service.'"

Interestingly, in spite of all the difficulty the Air Force had with its exception policy in the Matlovich case, the regulations adopted in 1981 still included an exception clause. According to the ACLU handbook, "A person may stay in the military, even though he or she has committed, or attempted to commit, a homosexual act, as long as the following conditions are met: if the act was a 'departure from the member's usual and customary behavior,' was done without 'force, coercion, or intimidation,' and is 'unlikely to recur,' if the member 'does not desire to engage in or intend to engage in [further] homosexual acts,' and if 'the member's continued presence in the Service is deemed consistent with the interest of the Service in proper discipline, good order, and morale.'" While this might seem to be creating a giant loophole by allowing the retention of those convicted of homosexual acts, the new regulations would still protect the military from the claims of an openly gay person like Matlovich, who, when he was in the Air Force, had every intention to engage in further homosexual acts, which to him *were* his "usual and customary behavior."

Ironically, at approximately the same time that these regulations were issued, the Air Force stopped asking prospective enlistees whether they had ever had homosexual tendencies. In June 1985, however, the Department of Defense issued a new application form to be used by all the services. On that form, which is still in use, question 37f asks, "Have you ever engaged in homosexual activity (sexual relations with another person of the same sex)?" Question 37 also asks about drug and alcohol use as well as "mental, nervous, emotional, psychological, or personality disorders." If an enlistee had any doubts regarding the military's attitude toward homosexuality, question 37f made it clear: none of the above need apply.

Still, gay people do apply, of course, and still, they fight to stay in. Petty Officer Dennis Beller, a Navy weatherman stationed in Monterey, California, was one of the first to follow Matlovich's example by challenging the military in court. Unlike Leonard, however, he did not voluntarily disclose his homosexuality. He was forced to do so as a result of an investigation by the FBI.

Beller had joined the Navy in 1960 and was living quietly with his lover, a former Marine, when the Navy decided that he required top secret security clearance. In the course of the investigation which followed, FBI agents asked questions about Beller's private life and discovered not only that he was living with a male lover but also that he had engaged in homosexual activity while stationed in Taiwan. Later, they tracked him to a gay bar in Monterey called the Gilded Cage.

After obtaining a sworn statement from Beller acknowledging his homosexuality, the Navy discharged him in April 1976. Beller promptly filed suit in the U.S. District Court in San Francisco, charging the Navy with violation of privacy and of his constitutional rights. The District Court entered judgment for the Navy, claiming that Beller knew the rules regarding homosexual conduct and must therefore live with the consequences. However, at the same time, Judge George Harris pointed to Beller's outstanding service record and declared, "The Navy does itself and the public little good by removing [such] an experienced and able serviceman . . . from its ranks, and it should seriously consider what interest is furthered by its decision to do so."

Beller appealed to the Ninth Circuit Court of Appeals in San Francisco, but in 1980 the court ruled that Beller's discharge did not violate his constitutional rights and that the Navy did indeed have the right to discharge personnel for homosexual conduct. According to Judge Anthony Kennedy, who wrote the opinion for the court (and who was later promoted to the Supreme Court), "While it is clear that one does not surrender his or her constitutional rights upon entering the military, the Supreme Court has repeatedly held that constitutional rights must be viewed in light of the special circumstances and needs of the armed forces."

One of these needs is the need to maintain discipline and order, noted Kennedy. Yet, "despite the evidence that attitudes towards homosexual conduct have changed among some groups in society, the Navy could conclude that a substantial number of naval personnel have feelings regarding homosexuality, based upon moral precepts recognized by many in our society as legitimate, which would create tensions and hostilities."

Another concern of the court was that the Navy not be forced to "condone" homosexual behavior. If the Navy were forced to alter its regulations, said Kennedy, "The Navy . . . could conclude rationally that toleration of homosexual conduct, as expressed in a less broad prohibition, might be understood as tacit approval."

Continued the judge, "In view of the importance of the military's role, the special need for discipline and order in the service, the potential for difficulties arising out of possible close confinement aboard ships or bases for long periods of time, and the possible benefit to recruiting efforts . . . , we conclude that at the present time the regulation represents a reasonable effort to accommodate the needs of the Government with the interests of the individual."

Nevertheless, Kennedy tempered his ruling by noting, "Upholding the challenged regulations as constitutional is distinct from a statement that they are wise. The latter judgment is neither implicit in our decision nor within our province to make. . . . We are mindful that the rule discharging these plaintiffs is a harsh one in their individual cases, but we cannot under the guise of due process give our opinion on the fairness of every application of the military regulation." He added that Supreme Court precedents "suggest that some kinds of government regulation of private consensual homosexual behavior may face substantial constitutional challenge." In any case, Kennedy concluded, "The Navy's blanket rule requiring discharge of all who have engaged in homsexual conduct is perhaps broader than necessary to accomplish some of its goals."

With help from the National Gay Rights Advocates, Beller and his lawyer once again appealed the case, this time to the Supreme Court. Beller sought back pay and reinstatement. However, in June 1981, the Court refused to hear the appeal. With no options left, Beller left the Navy and became a computer operator for a firm in Sunnyvale.

While Judge Kennedy noted that his decision was a narrow one and that there might be constitutional rights for gay people in other areas and contexts, the next case involving gay people in the military to garner national attention did not even achieve this much. This case involved a twenty-seven-year-old Navy petty officer, also stationed in Monterey, named James Dronenburg, who was discharged in 1981 as a result of a series of investigations that he described as a "witch hunt." The Navy, on the basis of allegations by a nineteen-year-old seaman, charged Dronenburg with repeatedly engaging in homosexual conduct in a Navy barracks while studying at the Defense Language Institute — charges which Dronenburg first denied but later acknowledged.

After his discharge, Dronenburg filed a suit against the Navy, claiming violation of his constitutional right to privacy and equal protection of the laws. Federal District Judge Oliver Gasch felt otherwise, however, and rejected his suit. The case then went to the Court of Appeals for the District of Columbia, where Judge Robert Bork, the man whose eventual nomination to the Supreme Court by President Reagan was rejected by the Senate, joined future Supreme Court Justice Antonin Scalia and Judge David W. Williams of Los Angeles in upholding the lower court decision in August 1984.

For the court, Judge Bork wrote an opinion that was excoriated by gay rights activists and civil libertarians across the nation. After lauding Dronenburg for his "unblemished service record" and his "many citations praising his job performance in nine years as a Korean linguist and cryptographer" with a top secret security clearance, Bork nevertheless rejected Dronenburg's claim that his rights had been violated. There was no equal rights violation, wrote Bork, because the Navy policy "is plainly a rational means of advancing a legitimate, indeed a crucial, common interest to all our armed forces." He continued, "The effects of homosexual conduct within a naval or military unit are almost certain to he harmful to morale and discipline." Like Kennedy, Bork made a specific reference to other servicemen who "find homosexuality morally offensive." He also brought up "the possibility of homosexual seduction" involving officers and enlisted men.

Addressing Dronenburg's other claim, his right to privacy, Bork stated that this right was not violated, for "private, consensual homosexual conduct is not constitutionally protected. . . . [The Supreme Court] has never defined the right [of privacy] so broadly as to encompass homosexual conduct." For a precedent, he pointed to the Supreme Court's 1976 decision summarily affirming a lower court decision upholding Virginia's sodomy laws, which make private consensual homosexual acts a crime.

Reaching further afield, Bork stated that "legislation may implement morality" in sexual matters and that the courts had no right to expand constitutional rights regarding sexual activity. "It [is] impossible to conclude," Bork wrote, "that a right to homosexual conduct is 'fundamental' or 'implicit in the concept of ordered liberty' unless any and all private sexual behavior falls within those categories, a conclusion we are unwilling to draw. . . . If the revolution in sexual mores that appellant proclaims is in fact ever to arrive, we think it must arrive through the moral choices of the people and their elected representatives, not through the judicial ukase of this court."

Reaction from the gay community and their supporters was fast and furious. The National Gay Task Force issued a statement calling the decision "a threat to all Americans." David Addlestone, Matlovich's attorney, called it "flaming babble." Frank Kameny found it a "venemous decision [which was] a launching pad for a horrendous anti-gay tirade. It was an assault on the whole concept of gay rights." Agreed Leonard Graff of the National Gay Rights Advocates, "I feel that Bork over-reached himself. He went far beyond what he needed to decide the case." Looking to the future, the Bar Association for Human Rights of Greater New York asserted, "The D.C. Circuit decision is so broad in its sweep as to have repercussions far beyond the narrow question of the military regulations."

Beller and *Dronenburg* notwithstanding, not all the major court challenges ended in defeat. Miriam ben-Shalom joined the Army Reserves in 1974 in Milwaukee but was processed for discharge the following year because she was an open lesbian. Like Matlovich, Beller, and Dronenburg, she was a fine soldier. She consistently received outstanding reviews from her superiors. This did her no good with the Army brass, however, and in 1976, with a year left on her enlistment contract, she was discharged from the service.

In 1978, ben-Shalom and her lawyer, Steven Glenn, filed a court case. Two years later, Judge Terrance Evans of the Eastern District Court of Wisconsin issued a summary judgment in her behalf, ordering her reinstatement on the grounds that her First Amendment rights — specifically, her right to free speech — had been violated. While Judge Evans agreed with the Army that it is not a right but a privilege to serve in the Armed Forces, he added that this does not give the military the authority to withhold the right of free speech. However, he did not acknowledge any specific constitutional right that guaranteed ben-Shalom protection from discrimination as a homosexual.

The Army immediately filed a notice of appeal but later dismissed it. Instead, it claimed that during the pendency of the court case ben-Shalom's enlistment contract had expired. It therefore considered itself obligated only to give her back pay but not to re-enlist her. In the meantime, ben-Shalom had no way to enforce Judge Evans' decision, for her attorney, who had been working for her pro bono, withdrew from the case. For three years, nothing happened.

In 1983, however, ben-Shalom retained another attorney, who filed a motion for contempt against the Army in 1984, claiming that the Army was remiss in not reinstating ben-Shalom after all this time. At the contempt hearing, the same judge who heard the case originally, Judge Evans, found that contempt against the Army hadn't been proved because the Army claimed it was willing to negotiate a monetary settlement with ben-Shalom. Evans then ordered the Army to give ben-Shalom less than one thousand dollars in back pay but reversed himself on the reinstatement matter.

With yet another attorney, Mark Rogers, ben-Shalom appealed this decision to the Seventh Circuit Court of Appeals in 1984. That court upheld Evans's finding that the Army was not in contempt but added that the judge had overreached his powers when he stripped ben-Shalom of her judgment for reinstatement. In the fall of 1985, Rogers's associate, Patrick Berigan, filed a motion to enforce the judgment. The Army appealed, and following yet another round of legal maneuvering, the Seventh Circuit ruled conclusively in ben-Shalom's favor in August 1987. The Army was forced to reinstate her effective September 1.

In the spring of 1988, ben-Shalom made a formal request for re-enlistment. On May 1, however, she was informed by her superior officers that she was being barred once again because of her homosexuality. The Army claimed it had this right because the court order reinstating ben-Shalom was based primarily on her First Amendment right to *say* she was a lesbian and not on any alleged constitutional right to *be* one.

As noted above, the old regulations said nothing about service members who professed to be homosexuals; it only concerned those who engaged in homosexual acts. The Army never did prove that ben-Shalom ever engaged in any lesbian acts. In their view, this was why they lost the case. Under the regulations adopted in 1981, however, the Army felt it had no need to establish homosexual conduct, simply orientation. Until the celebrated Perry Watkins decision in February 1988, no appellate level court had ever ruled that gay service members — even if they were celibate — had a constitutional right to equal protection.

Ben-Shalom responded by filing suit against the military and requesting injunctive relief (i.e., requesting that an injunction be issued to prevent the Army from denying her re-enlistment based on her sexual preference). The case was assigned to Judge Myron L. Gordon of the Eastern District of Wisconsin. On August 3, 1988, he issued this preliminary injunction, ordering the Army to consider her re-enlistment request absent any consideration of sexual preference, pending further decision of the court. The Army refused to do this and chose to extend her old service contract instead. Because this would have prevented ben-Shalom from being promoted or becoming a drill instructor at the leadership academy, this was unacceptable to her. Her lawyers filed a motion for contempt.

In September, Judge Evans found the Army in contempt for violating the preliminary injunction order and ordered them to re-enlist ben-Shalom without further delay or pay a penalty of one thousand dollars a day. The Army had no choice but to comply. As a result, ben-Shalom is currently a member of the 84th Division while waiting for a final decision from Judge Gordon. Whatever Gordon decides will surely be influenced by the Perry Watkins case, which, in early 1988, set new precedents concerning gay people and the military.

Watkins was drafted into the Army in 1967, during the height of the war in Vietnam, when he was nineteen. He was drafted even though he told an Army psychiatrist at his pre-induction physical that he was gay and had been ever since the age of thirteen. On several other occasions he acknowledged his homosexuality without jeopardizing his career. In 1968 he told an Army Criminal Division investigator that he was gay and that he had engaged in homosexual relations with two servicemen. A re-enlistment review of his records in 1975 again brought the matter to the attention of his superiors. Nevertheless, he was deemed "suitable for retention in the military."

For nearly fifteen years, the Army allowed Watkins to serve. His record was outstanding. One commanding officer called him "one of our most respected and trusted soldiers." However, in 1979, following a tour of duty in Europe, where Watkins served with the Nuclear Surety Personnel Reliability Program, the Army took away his security clearance. After Watkins protested this revocation, and following the implementation of its new regulations in 1981, the Army refused his request for re-enlistment, citing his "self-admitted homosexuality."

Watkins sued, and in 1982 in Seattle, District Court Judge Barbara Rothstein ruled in his favor. She said that the Army's contention that it did not know he was gay was "patently absurd," given his openness over the years. Having given him a number of "green lights," it could not then discharge him.

A year later, however, a three-judge panel of the Ninth Circuit Court of Appeals in San Francisco ruled unanimously to overturn the lower court order. Noted Judge Herbert Choy, who wrote the opinion for the court, the lower court had "in effect ordered military officials to violate their own regulations" by ordering them to retain Watkins. Choy continued that the court had no power to force them to do this unless those regulations are proven to be "repugnant to the Constituition or to statutory authority. That is not the case here." Furthermore, Choy added, the court would not rule on any constitutional question, for Watkins' case was not the kind in which federal civilian courts have jurisdiction.

However, in a concurring opinion that was called a "stinging rebuke" to the Army by the *San Francisco Chronicle*, Judge William Norris criticized the current Army regulation against gay service members as a "regressive policy [which] demonstrates a callous disregard for the progress American law and society have made toward acknowledging that an individual's choice of lifestyle is not the concern of government, but a fundamental aspect of personal liberty." Because of this policy, the judge concluded, "Our nation has lost a fine soldier and Sergeant Watkins has suffered a manifest injustice."

After reversing the lower court decision, the appeals court sent the case back to Judge Rothstein for further consideration. Years later, in February 1988, after the usual legal maneuvers and delays, he won a stunning victory. The U.S. Court of Appeals in San Francisco ruled two to one that the Army's prohibition of homosexuals was unconstitutional on the grounds of equal protection. It was the first time ever that a federal appellate court extended constitutional protection to homosexuals in the military.

Writing for the majority, Judge William Norris noted that the Army's concerns about morale and discipline "illegitimately cater to private biases." Gay soldiers, he said, are entitled to the same protection from discrimination as other racial minorities: "The discrimination faced by homosexuals in our society is plainly no less pernicious or intense than the discrimination faced by other groups already treated as suspect classes, such as aliens or people of a particular national origin. ... Laws that limit the acceptable focus of one's sexual desires to members of the opposite sex, like laws that limit one's choice of spouse (or sexual partner) to members of the same race, cannot withstand constitutional scrutiny absent a compelling governmental justification."

Furthermore, Norris said, the Army's justification that homosexuals would hurt military morale and discipline was just as absurd as its previous claims that integration would do the same. "For much of our history, the military's fear of racial tension kept black soldiers separated from whites. Today it is unthinkable that the judiciary would defer to the Army's prior 'professional' judgment that black and white soldiers had to be segregated to avoid interracial tensions."

Acknowledging the Supreme Court's infamous *Bowers v. Hardwick* decision of 1986, in which the Court upheld the Georgia sodomy law, Norris drew a clear distinction between homosexual conduct and homosexual orientation. He said that just because specific sexual conduct can be forbidden by criminal laws, this does not mean that those laws can be considered "a state license to pass 'homosexual laws' — laws imposing special restrictions on gays because they are gay." Norris also referred to the Army's 1981 regulations, which make the same distinction between homosexual conduct and orientation but condemn both. Regarding the Army's exception policy, Norris said, "If a straight soldier and a gay soldier of the same sex engage in homosexual acts because they are drunk, immature, or curious, the straight soldier may remain in the Army while the gay soldier is automatically terminated. In short, the regulations do not penalize soldiers for engaging in homosexual acts; they penalize soldiers who have engaged in homosexual acts only when the Army decides those soldiers are actually gay."

Dissenting Judge Stephen Reinhardt departed from the majority reluctantly. "Were I free to apply my own view of the meaning of the Constitution and in that light pass upon the validity of the Army's regulations, I too would conclude that the Army may not refuse to enlist homosexuals," said Reinhardt. However, he felt bound by the *Hardwick* case, which compelled him to vote in favor of the Army's regulations. Nevertheless, he added, "Before concluding my discussion of *Hardwick*, I wish to record my own view of the opinion. . . . As I understand our Constitution, a state simply has no business treating any group of persons as the State of Georgia and other states with sodomy statutes treat homosexuals. . . . I believe that the Supreme Court egregiously misinterpreted the Constitution in *Hardwick*. In my view, *Hardwick* improperly condones official bias and prejudice against homosexuals, and authorizes the criminalization of conduct that is an essential part of the intimate sexual life of our many homosexual citizens, a group that has historically been the victim of unfair and irrational treatment. . . . I am confident that, in the long run, *Hardwick* will be overruled by a wiser and more enlightened Court."

With such a decision (and, indeed, even such a dissenting opinion), gay leaders were ecstatic. Said Leonard Graff of the National Gay Rights Advocates, "There is a huge outpouring of support for the ruling. It's a tremendous victory for the constitutional rights of gays all over the country. . . . It's about time that the courts recognized that gay people have been denied their rights. . . . The case will have far-reaching effects. We're very excited about it." Added Mary Dunlap, a lesbian civil rights lawyer based in San Francisco, "This decision is totally and thoroughly ground-breaking." Watkins's lawyer, James Lobsenz of the ACLU agreed and added, "We're extremely pleased by Judge Norris's decision and we think that finally we have a court that recognizes this type of discrimination is incompatible with the fundamental rights guaranteed by the Constitution."

Whether or not the Ninth Circuit decision will stand, however, remains to be seen. Soon after it was issued, the Reagan administration, disturbed that the ruling was made by a panel consisting of three of the most liberal judges in the circuit, requested that the circuit reconsider its decision *en banc*. In June 1988, a majority of the thirty-three circuit judges agreed. Because the Ninth Circuit is the largest in the nation, this means that a panel of eleven judges rather than all thirty-three would hear the case.

On October 12, 1988, ACLU attorney Lobsenz again argued Watkins's case before the Ninth Circuit. The court has yet to issue its decision. Even if the court decides in Watkins's favor, however, the battle may continue. The Army would almost certainly appeal the case to the U.S. Supreme Court, where the conservative majority could very well overturn the appellate court decision. David Addlestone warned in early 1988, "As I've told other lawyers involved in similar cases, you're really playing with fire when you take cases like this to the courts. Once you start litigating things in the military context, you're really asking for trouble. It's an awful arena for civil rights issues. The courts can backfire on you, and you can create a political movement in the other direction. . . . If the Supreme Court does get its hands on this case, it's likely to be a disaster. I just think people have to bite the bullet and say if you're gay in the military you're going to have to do it in the closet."

Despite Addlestone's warnings, the man who started it all, Leonard Matlovich, was too excited about the Watkins case when he heard about it to worry about future Supreme Court decisions. But Matlovich was always an optimist. Even before the Watkins decision, he said:

"After my case there was a rash of similar cases. None of them have succeeded yet, but we shouldn't expect them to. There isn't going to be any one case. There are going to be many cases. It's going to be a very slow process, and we have to understand that. Blacks fought for over a hundred years before *Brown v. the Board of Education*. But as long as we are patient, we'll get there.

"That doesn't mean that equal rights will automatically lead to acceptance, though. In the military, for instance, you can control people's behavior through regulations, but you can't necessarily control their attitudes. If you have the law on your side, of course, that helps, and one day we will have the law on our side. But we will still need to change attitudes by coming out of the closet to family and friends. This will require a sacrifice. We simply have to be willing to flaunt our virtues. You can't discriminate against a virtuous person, after all. You can't deny the rights of someone who you know is contributing to society."

As far as Leonard Matlovich was concerned, Perry Watkins is one such "virtuous person" who has contributed greatly to society. Like so many others, he was elated about Watkins's victory:

"We all owe Perry Watkins a great deal of gratitude and respect for sticking with this thing and fighting for what he believes. He's truly a magnificent role model for all of us. His case is wonderful, incredible, long past due. It is the single most important decision ever rendered in the area of homosexual rights. It shows that perserverance pays off and that gays and lesbians have as much a right to serve in the military as anyone else.

"Until now, the military has always been considered outside the Constitution as a separate entity by the courts. But if the Supreme Court upholds this decision, it will in effect amend the '64 Civil Rights Act by adding homosexuality to the list. If it becomes unconstitutional for the military to discriminate against gay people, then it becomes unconstitutional for everyone in America to discriminate against gay people.

"If I had to make a prediction, I would say that the Supreme Court will decide by a five-to-four vote and that Kennedy will be the swing vote. Which way he will rule, however, I don't know. He ruled against us in the past. But he also is responsible for adding that famous footnote — that at some time in the future society is going to have to deal with homosexuality. Perhaps this is that time.

"Although I've never met Perry Watkins, I have no regrets that this decision is the result of his case and not mine. You have to understand that we are all dominos. Each case is a domino that knocks down the next. Even though I won my case on a technicality only, Mary Dunlap told me that I should take a lot of pride in this decision, because twelve years ago we were out there battling for it. And to be honest with you, this has happened a lot faster than I thought it would. I didn't think the courts were ready for this. It's incredible.

"As far as the future of gay people in the military is concerned, the military is just a mirror of society, so it will be what we're willing to make it. At present, of course, the military is fighting the court decision, but a long time ago I discovered something amazing about the military. For one hundred years it may fight something, but when it changes, it changes overnight. It's called the old boy network. If you want to get to the top, you've got to be an old boy, and all the old boys think alike. It's amazing how fast they all line up behind the boss. So once one man of courage decides to make a change regarding homosexuality, if he's in a position of leadership everything will change.

"Even if the old boys ignore our concerns, this decision will definitely change the military by putting homosexuality in a positive aspect for others. Take that high school kid who wants to join the military. When he sees the sentiments he learned in civics class — 'My country, 'tis of thee, sweet land of liberty' — validated by the courts and perhaps even put into practice, then maybe he'll believe in the principles of America. And so will we all."

172

INDEX

About the Author:

Mike Hippler is a San Francisco-based columnist whose news articles and commentary appear in newspapers and magazines across the nation. His regular column in the *Bay Area Reporter* has earned him three consecutive Cable Car Awards, and a place in their Hall of Honor. Covering the news had another unexpected bonus for Hippler — he met his lover when they both participated in the Supreme Court demonstration in Washington in October 1987.

Describing himself as having "a keen sense of history," Hippler feels that "Leonard Matlovich was one of the most visible leaders of the gay liberation movement in the 1970s. He also provided a voice that is not often heard in the gay community — proving that we do indeed come from every part of a very broad spectrum."

Matlovich: The Good Soldier is Hippler's first book.

Other books of interest from
ALYSON PUBLICATIONS

THE MEN WITH THE PINK TRIANGLE, by Heinz Heger. Translated by David Fernbach, $6.00. For decades, history ignored the Nazi persecution of gay people. Only with the rise of the gay movement in the 1970s did historians finally recognize that gay people, like Jews and others deemed "undesirable," suffered enormously at the hands of the Nazi regime. Of the few who survived the concentration camps, only one ever came forward to tell his story. His true account of those nightmarish years provides an important introduction to a long-forgotten chapter of gay history.

OUT OF ALL TIME, by Terry Boughner, $7.00. Historian Terry Boughner scans the centuries and picks out scores of the past's most celebrated gay, lesbian and bisexual personalities. From ancient Egypt to the twentieth century, from Alcibiades to Willa Cather, we discover a part of history that has too often been censored or ignored. Each chapter is imaginatively illustrated by *Washington Blade* caricaturist Michael Willhoite.

A HISTORY OF SHADOWS, by Robert C. Reinhart, $7.00. Through the eyes of four older gay men, Robert Reinhart vividly depicts what it was like to grow up gay in America a half-century ago, and to live in the closet during the Depression, World War II, the McCarthy period, and the Sixties.

WE CAN ALWAYS CALL THEM BULGARIANS, by Kaier Curtin, $10.00. In this landmark study, theater historian Kaier Curtin charts the struggle to portray the lives of gay men and lesbians on the American stage. Despite virulent homophobia, many plays with gay and lesbian characters did appear on Broadway in the first half of the twentieth century, and Curtin documents the controversies sparked by these works.

RAT AND THE DEVIL, by Louis Hyde, ed., $10.00. They met in 1924 — a middle-aged artist and a promising young graduate student. Over the next twenty years, Russell Cheney and F.O. Matthiessen, who became one of America's leading literary historians, forged a durable, loving relationship despite successful careers and long absences. In this series of over 3,000 letters, their story is told in their own words.

ULRICHS, by Hubert Kennedy, $9.00. Karl Heinrich Ulrichs became the first man in modern times to publicly speak out in favor of homosexual rights when he declared to a convention of German jurists in 1867 that he himself was an "Urning." He was also an activist and writer in an age when that meant standing alone. Here, in the first complete biography of this early pioneer, Hubert Kennedy describes the life and ideas of the man who laid the foundation for today's gay movement.

LONG TIME PASSING: Lives of Older Lesbians, by Marcy Adelman, ed., $8.00. Here, in their own words, women talk about age-related concerns: the fear of losing a lover; the experiences of being a lesbian in the 1940s and 1950s; and issues of loneliness and community.

THE GAY BOOK OF LISTS, by Leigh Rutledge, $7.00. Rutledge has compiled a fascinating and informative collection of lists. His subject matter ranges from history (6 gay popes) to politics (9 perfectly disgusting reactions to AIDS) to entertainment (12 examples of gays on network television) to humor (9 Victorian "cures" for masturbation). Learning about gay culture and history has never been so much fun.

UNNATURAL QUOTATIONS, by Leigh Rutledge, $8.00. The author of *The Gay Book of Lists* has been back digging through his files and has put together this entertaining collection of quotations by or about gay people. Well-illustrated and indexed for handy reference, *Unnatural Quotations* is another must for your bookshelf.

THE ALYSON ALMANAC, $7.00. Almanacs have been popular sources of information since "Poor Richard" first put thoughts on paper and Yankee farmers started forecasting the weather. Here is a sourcebook for gay men and lesbians that offers financial planning for same-sex couples, short biographies of nearly two-hundred gay people throughout history, unusual vacation ideas, and much, much more.

IN THE LIFE: A Black Gay Anthology, by Joseph Beam, ed., $8.00. When Joseph Beam became frustrated that so little gay male literature spoke to him as a black man, he decided to do something about it. The result is this anthology, in which 29 contributors, through stories, essays, verse and artwork, have made heard the voice of a too-often silent minority.

GOLDENBOY, by Michael Nava, $15.00 (cloth). Gay lawyer-sleuth Henry Rios returns, in a sequel to Nava's highly-praised *The Little Death.*
    Did Jim Pears kill the co-worker who threatened to expose his homosexuality? The evidence says so, but too many people *want* Pears to be guilty. Distracted by grisly murders and the glitz of Hollywood, can Rios prove his client's innocence?

REVELATIONS, Wayne Curtis, ed., $8.00. Twenty-two men, ranging in age from their teens to their seventies, tell their own coming out stories. No book has ever presented such a varied and personal look at coming out as a gay man in modern America.

TESTIMONIES, by Sarah Holmes, ed., $8.00. In this new collection of coming out stories, twenty-two women of widely varying backgrounds and ages give accounts of their journeys toward self-discovery.

SHADOWS OF LOVE, by Charles Jurrist, ed., $9.00. In this new short story anthology, editor Charles Jurrist displays the rich diversity of gay male writing in contemporary America. Among the sixteen authors represented in this collection are several previously unpublished writers, as well as the often-unheard voices of racial and ethnic minorities. These stories present fresh and unusual perspectives on the modern gay experience.

AS WE ARE, by Don Clark, $8.00. This book, from the author of *Loving Someone Gay* and *Living Gay*, examines our gay identity in the AIDS era. Clark explores the growth and maturation of the gay community in recent years. By breaking down our ability to love and care for one another into its components, Clark creates a clear picture of where we have been, where we are going, and he emphasizes the importance of being *As We Are.*

These titles are available at many bookstores, or by mail.

– — – — – — – — – — – — – — – — – — –

Enclosed is $_____ for the following books. (Add $1.00 postage when ordering just one book; if you order two or more, we'll pay the postage.)

1. _____   2. _____

3. _____   4. _____

5. _____   6. _____

name: _____ address:_____

city:_____ state:_____zip:_____

ALYSON PUBLICATIONS
Dept. H-29, 40 Plympton St., Boston, Mass. 02118

After Dec. 31, 1991, please write for current catalog.

Matlovich as a young boy. "We were very adventurous kids, always getting in trouble for going where we really shouldn't have been."

Matlovich and a date on the way to the Junior/Senior Prom. Often before leaving on dates he and his girlfriend would kneel on the floor and say the Rosary to protect themselves from sin.

As a high school senior, Matlovich was named "most talkative" boy. Although he met Leonard years later, Steve Pizzo remembered his "ever-happy, ever-smiling, ever-animated, never-at-a-loss-for-words character."

At nineteen, Matlovich was inducted into the Air Force with his father at his side. "I had to prove that even though I had strong attractions to other men, I could go to war just like anyone else."

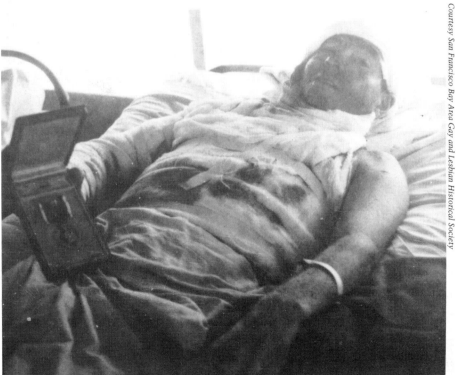

Matlovich received numerous citations and medals, but none that he cherished more — or earned more painfully — than his Purple Heart (lower photo). "I stuck my shovel in the ground, but it wouldn't stand up. So I gave it a harder push, and it blew up . . . my right lung was blown down into my stomach and I had holes all over me where the shrapnel went in."

Matlovich after his well-publicized coming out. "I found myself, little nobody me, standing up in front of tens of thousands of gay people. And just two years ago I thought I was the only gay in the world. It was a mixture of joy and sadness."

Matlovich used his speaking ability to promote the movement, and grew used to being interviewed. Michael Bedwell remarked that when Matlovich went on a television talk show, "the younger women wanted to marry him and the older women wanted to mother him. They certainly never reacted this way to other leaders of the movement." With Matlovich in the lower photo is Mike Hippler, author of this biography.

Matlovich in the last year of his life. "Since I've had AIDS I've seen so much to admire. We've developed so many support groups and buddy systems. For this much love, care, and compassion to come out of this community proves that we truly are people of incredible love. We're going to be a better community because of this."

Matlovich and his gay veterans' memorial. The tombstone simply reads, "A Gay Vietnam Veteran." This is followed by a statement: "When I was in the military they gave me a medal for killing two men and a discharge for loving one." Matlovich was later buried in this plot.

The author would like to express appreciation for the cooperation of the San Francisco Bay Area Gay and Lesbian Historical Society, which provided many of the photographs for this book.

Those interested in donating materials, or who would like to consult the Matlovich Papers, should write to:

Archivist
SFBAGLHS
PO Box 42126
San Francisco, CA
94142